"You will marry me, Abby," Cash said, his eyes glinting dangerously.

Abby had known that Cash would demand marriage. What she hadn't expected was to hear him speak so calmly of divorce.

She edged around him. "So you're not talking about a *real* marriage. Just a marriage on paper. So that when our child asks about it later, it'll look like we cared."

Cash frowned. "That's not what I said. I said we'd try."

"*Try,*" Abby snapped. "There's a puny little word."

"Abby, you're fifteen years younger than I am! And you said yourself that we're neither of us the marrying kind. We haven't a snowflake's chance in hell of making a marriage last! But I want to do right by you and my baby."

He grasped her shoulders, and Abby felt his strength. "Say yes, Abby," he growled.

And Abby knew that, whatever Cash Bravo asked…she would always say yes.

D0949176

Dear Reader,

Happy New Year! We look forward to bringing you another year of captivating, deeply satisfying romances that will surely melt your heart!

January's THAT SPECIAL WOMAN! title revisits the Window Rock community for the next installment of Cheryl Reavis's FAMILY BLESSINGS miniseries. *Tenderly* is about a vulnerable young woman's quest to uncover her heritage— and the once-in-a-lifetime love she discovers with a brave Navajo police officer. Don't miss this warm, wonderful story!

It's a case of unrequited love—or is it?—in *The Nine-Month Marriage*, the first story in Christine Rimmer's delightful new series, CONVENIENTLY YOURS. This starry-eyed heroine can't believe her ears when the man she worships proposes a marriage—even if it's just for their baby's sake. And the red-hot passion continues when a life-threatening crisis brings a tempestuous couple together in *Little Boy Blue* by Suzannah Davis—book three in the SWITCHED AT BIRTH miniseries.

Also this month, fate reunites a family in *A Daddy for Devin* by Jennifer Mikels. And an unlikely duo find solace in each other's arms when they are snowbound together, but a secret threatens to drive them apart in *Her Child's Father* by Christine Flynn. We finish off the month with a poignant story about a heroine who falls in love with her ex-groom's brother, but her child's paternity could jeopardize their happiness in *Brother of the Groom* by Judith Yates.

I hope this New Year brings you much health and happiness! Enjoy this book and all our books to come!

Sincerely,

Tara Gavin
Senior Editor and Editorial Coordinator

Please address questions and book requests to:
Silhouette Reader Service
U.S.: 3010 Walden Ave., P.O. Box 1325, Buffalo, NY 14269
Canadian: P.O. Box 609, Fort Erie, Ont. L2A 5X3

CHRISTINE RIMMER

THE NINE-MONTH MARRIAGE

SPECIAL EDITION®

Published by Silhouette Books
America's Publisher of Contemporary Romance

For Phylis Warady.
Thanks, Phyl, for the tea and the company,
the funny stories, the kind words and
the thoughtful advice—
not to mention watering my houseplants
and taking care of Jesse's lizard.
You are a treasure.

 SILHOUETTE BOOKS

ISBN 0-373-24148-8

THE NINE-MONTH MARRIAGE

Copyright © 1998 by Christine Rimmer

All rights reserved. Except for use in any review, the reproduction
or utilization of this work in whole or in part in any form by any
electronic, mechanical or other means, now known or hereafter
invented, including xerography, photocopying and recording, or in
any information storage or retrieval system, is forbidden without
the written permission of the editorial office, Silhouette Books,
300 East 42nd Street, New York, NY 10017 U.S.A.

All characters in this book have no existence outside the imagination of
the author and have no relation whatsoever to anyone bearing the same
name or names. They are not even distantly inspired by any individual
known or unknown to the author, and all incidents are pure invention.

This edition published by arrangement with Harlequin Books S.A.

® and TM are trademarks of Harlequin Books S.A., used under license.
Trademarks indicated with ® are registered in the United States Patent
and Trademark Office, the Canadian Trade Marks Office and in other
countries.

Printed in U.S.A.

Books by Christine Rimmer

Silhouette Special Edition

Double Dare #646
Slow Larkin's Revenge #698
Earth Angel #719
*Wagered Woman #794
Born Innnocent #833
*Man of the Mountain #886
*Sweetbriar Summit #896
* A Home for the Hunter #908
For the Baby's Sake #925
**Sunshine and the
   Shadowmaster* #979
**The Man, The Moon
   and The Marriage Vow* #1010
*No Less Than a Lifetime #1040
*Honeymoon Hotline #1063
*†The Nine-Month
   Marriage* #1148

Silhouette Desire

No Turning Back #418
Call It Fate #458
Temporary Temptress #602
Hard Luck Lady #640
Midsummer Madness #729
Counterfeit Bride #812
Cat's Cradle #940
*The Midnight Rider
   Takes a Bride* #1101

Silhouette Books

Fortune's Children
Wife Wanted

*The Jones Gang
†Conveniently Yours

CHRISTINE RIMMER

came to her profession the long way around. Before settling down to write about the magic of romance, she'd been an actress, a sales clerk, a janitor, a model, a phone sales representative, a teacher, a waitress, a playwright and an office manager. Now that she's finally found work that suits her perfectly, she insists she never had a problem keeping a job—she was merely gaining "life experience" for her future as a novelist. Those who know her best withhold comment when she makes such claims; they are grateful that she's at last found steady work. Christine is grateful, too—not only for the joy she finds in writing, but for what waits when the day's work is through: a man she loves who loves her right back, and the privilege of watching their children grow and change day to day. She lives with her family in Oklahoma.

THE BRAVOS

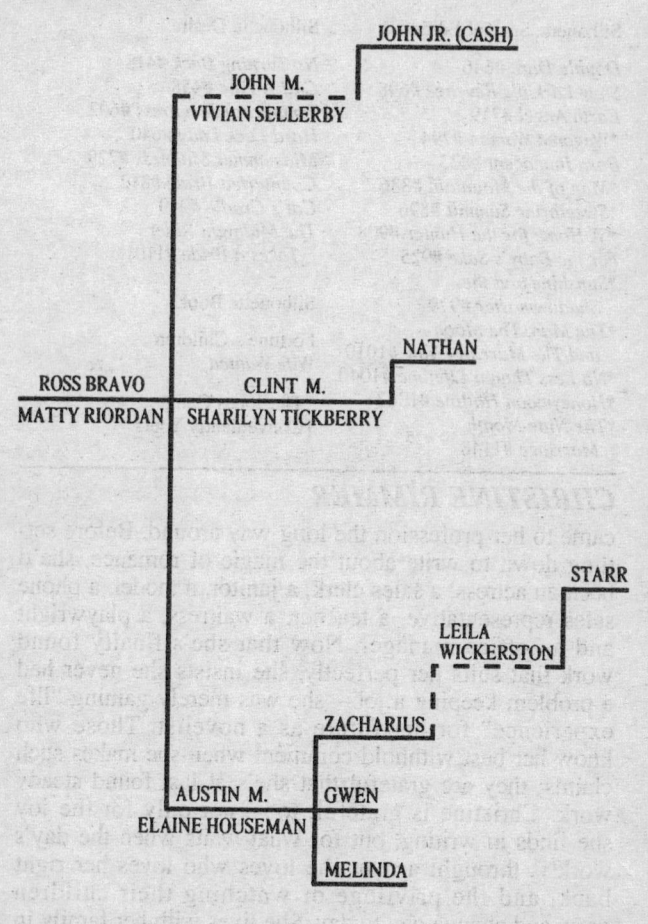

JOHN JR. (CASH)

JOHN M.
VIVIAN SELLERBY

NATHAN

ROSS BRAVO   CLINT M.
MATTY RIORDAN   SHARILYN TICKBERRY

STARR

LEILA
WICKERSTON

ZACHARIUS

AUSTIN M.   GWEN
ELAINE HOUSEMAN

MELINDA

(Broken lines indicate previous marriages)

Chapter One

Abby Heller heard a buzzing sound. She rolled to her back and opened one eye. It was light in the room: definitely morning. Not that Abby cared. She'd been up until three.

The buzzer sounded again. Abby put it together; there was someone at the door.

"Go away," she whispered at the faint watermark on the ceiling. Then she pulled the covers over her head.

Again, the buzzer sounded, like some irritating electronic sheep: "Baaaaaaa!"

And then it happened: everything in Abby's stomach started to rise.

She stuck out a hand, groping for the saltines on the cluttered table by the bed. At the same time she sucked in air slowly, and then slowly let it out.

A pocket calculator and an empty Dr Pepper bottle clattered to the carpet before her fingers closed on the waxed-paper wrapper. She pushed the covers off her face and dragged herself to a sitting position. Still breathing with great care, she fumbled with the roll of crackers.

"Baaaaaa!"

Her stomach roiled. She shot a look of absolute loathing at the scarred wooden door of her furnished studio apartment. And then, with grim determination, she stuck a cracker in her mouth. Slowly she chewed, taking long, careful breaths at the same time. She swallowed with caution, stuck in another cracker and chewed some more. The feeling that she would lose the contents of her stomach began to subside.

She got the second cracker down—and dared to hope it would be okay, that she wouldn't spend the next fifteen minutes hugging the bathroom fixtures after all.

"Baaaaaa!" the buzzer bleated again. And then a fist hit the door—three sharp raps.

She shot a glance at the clock by the bed. When she saw the time, she let out a sound so low and ominous it could only be called a snarl. Whoever had come pounding on her door at 7 a.m. was going to regret it.

Muttering an oath that would have made her mother furious, Abby tossed the crackers on the nightstand, threw back the covers and stalked across the room to the door. She looked through the peephole.

And saw Cash Bravo on the other side.

"Oh, God," she breathed in horror. Her stomach lurched. She pressed her hand to her mouth.

Miraculously, she didn't throw up.

His fist hit the door again. The buzzer buzzed, "Baaa—baaa—baaaaa!" And Cash called out, "Abby! I know you're in there. Come on. Open up."

For a moment, she considered grabbing her car keys and heading for the service porch off of her minuscule kitchenette. She could be down the back stairs before he realized she'd gone. The big T-shirt she'd slept in might not be appropriate for day wear, but it was decent enough for a drive in the car.

But then she shook her head. Running would get her nowhere. If Cash Bravo wanted to find her, he would.

No. Better to face him down and get it over with.

"Abby! Now!"

The hard command in his voice told her more than she wanted to know. If she didn't do something, he would beat the door down.

"Just a minute!"

She flew to the bathroom door and snatched her robe from the nail there. She shoved her arms in it, then knotted the belt. Then, turning, she caught a glimpse of herself in the streaked mirror over the bureau next to her bed.

A miserable groan escaped her. She looked awful, her skin pasty, her hair all tangled and lank. Ugly dark splotches marred the skin under her eyes. Oh, she didn't want him to see her like this! Partly because of stupid pride. And partly because he might guess—

She did not allow her mind to complete the thought. He was not going to guess. No one would know until she was ready—especially not Cash. And if he started in about how bad she looked, she would tell him she was just tired, from working so late.

"Abby!" He buzzed for the umpteenth time—and then he did a little more pounding for good measure.

"Coming..." The room was a mess, her clothes and books and shoes scattered everywhere. She'd always been that way: someone with places to go and things to do and no time for keeping house. For once, though, she wished she had a moment to—

"Abby!"

"All right!"

She marched to the door, yanked it open—and utterly despised herself for the hard fist of longing that closed around her heart as her eyes met his.

He stared for a moment, then muttered accusingly, "You look like hell."

She decided the best way to handle that remark was not to dignify it with an answer. Besides, he didn't look so great himself. His bronze skin had a gray cast to it. She would bet he'd kept some bartender real busy last night.

"Are you going to let me in?" Without waiting for an answer, he moved toward her. She stepped back, clearing the doorway—and gaining a little distance from him. She didn't want to be too near him, to feel the warmth he radiated or to smell the scent of his skin.

His sky blue eyes surveyed her poor little room. She tried not to grit her teeth as she watched him. She knew his every expression. Right then, his jaw looked like granite and his mouth made a flat line; he was dismissing everything that he saw.

When he was through looking around, he turned to her. "What's going on?"

She backed up a few more steps—until she bumped into the end of the bed. "What do you mean?"

"You know damn well what I mean. Spring semester ended weeks ago. And you're here in Denver instead of home where you belong. Why?"

"Cash, look—"

"We've called. Both your mother and me. Left message after message. But you never call back."

"Cash—"

"Why?"

She stared at him, aching with the sudden foolish need to launch herself at him, to feel his strong arms go around her. And to tell him everything, all of it—including how scared she was, and how tired. But of course she couldn't do that, couldn't go running to Cash this time, as she'd done all of her life until now. Now Cash himself was the problem—or at least a major part of it.

She folded her arms over her stomach, hunched her shoulders and tried to speak calmly. "I just...I wanted a change." It came out sounding almost as pitiful and lost as she felt.

His eyes seemed to bore right down into the center of her. "You never wanted a change before."

"Well, now I do." Her robe had fallen open a little in front. She straightened it, avoiding those eyes.

She heard him sigh. He was turning away when she looked up, alligator boots striding across the worn gray carpet, moving toward the arch that framed her kitchenette.

In front of the arch stood a Formica-topped table, on which Abby had set up her computer. Cash dropped into one of the table's three chairs, leaned back and scrubbed both hands down his face. "It's all my fault, isn't it?"

"No. Of course not."

He lowered his hands. Their gazes locked. "Abby, you never were a very good liar. Just lay it out like it is, all right? You don't want to come home because of me, because of what happened."

He looked so utterly miserable. Longing squeezed her heart again, hard and painfully sweet—to go to him, to pull him close, to run her fingers through his silky dark-gold hair.

But she stayed where she was. And she spoke in careful, reasonable tones. "It's not your fault. Or at least, it's no more your fault than mine."

"But it *is* the reason you won't come home."

She dropped to the end of the bed. "Cash, I need some time. Please understand. I need to think things through."

He shoved a stack of accounting books aside, making room to rest an elbow on the table's edge. "I don't want this for you." He gestured broadly. "Living in a place like this. Working in some cheap bar."

She sat up straighter. "How do you know where I work?"

He just looked at her.

She thought of Nate. Nate Bravo was Cash's cousin, but they were more like brothers, really. Nate was a private investigator. "Nate?" she demanded, anger sparking. "You put Nate on me?"

He shook his head. "Uh-uh. I followed you myself. Last night. Then I went back to my hotel and got blasted. And then this morning, well...here I am."

It all seemed so pitiful. "Oh, Cash...."

"You're just a kid. And I know you looked up to me. *Trusted* me..."

She hated the self-loathing in his voice. She wanted to yell at him, to demand that he stop blaming himself. But at least one of them had to remain reasonable. "Cash, I'm twenty-one years old. Not as ancient as you are, maybe. But old enough to take responsibility for my own actions. I don't blame you, honestly."

He leaned toward her, hope kindling in his eyes. "Then come home to Medicine Creek where you belong. Work for me through the summer, the way you always have. That *is* what we agreed."

"Cash—"

"No. Listen. Remember." He spoke with such urgency, as if he really believed that she needed reminding of the things they had said, as if reminding her would make her abide by them. "You told me you'd go back to Boulder, finish out your semester. And then you were supposed to come home. We said that we were going to put what happened behind us. And we can do that. I know it. We can make things the way they used to be."

She gazed at his beloved face, thinking that maybe *he* could go back, but she couldn't. Not ever.

Until that night two months before, Cash had been her best friend. He had been like a big brother, yes—someone who looked out for her, someone who wanted to help make all her dreams come true. But there had been even more than that. They'd shared something so special. They had been true comrades, in spite of the difference in their ages.

But now, everything had changed. Now, if she let herself be near him, she'd end up just like every other woman he knew, looking at him with hungry eyes, mooning after him all day long. She didn't think she could bear that. She had better things to do with herself than moon after a man—even if that man was Cash.

"Come home," he said again.

She drew back her shoulders and spoke with finality. "No, Cash. I'm sorry, but I can't go home now."

He scowled at her. She didn't waver. And then his eyes narrowed. "Is there something you should tell me about?"

Though her pulse shot into overdrive and sweat broke out under her arms, she neither blinked nor shuddered. "Like what?"

"Abby, we weren't..." His cheeks puffed as he blew out a breath. "Careful. And it *was* your first time."

She looked away, toward the door, praying he would just let it go.

Her prayer got her nowhere. He forged on.

"You weren't using anything—you couldn't have been. And me, well, I acted like a damn fool all the way around."

She continued looking toward the door.

"Just tell me. Are you pregnant?"

It was the moment. The moment to say it. But she simply could not deal with having him know. Not right then. Not yet....

So she turned her head, looked him right in the eye and told a whopper of a lie. "No."

His big body visibly relaxed. "Well. At least we don't have to face a disaster like that."

"Yes." Her voice sounded funny, pinched and tight. She coughed to loosen her throat. "At least not that."

There was a pencil on the table, next to the stack of accounting books. He grabbed it, began idly tapping it on the tabletop, his watchful eyes studying her at the same time. Then all at once, he tossed the pencil down and stood. "You're too skinny. Get dressed. We'll get some breakfast into you."

Breakfast was the last thing she wanted to deal with right then. "No, Cash. Really, I—"

"Don't argue. I plan to stick around this town for a few days. I want to make sure you're going to be all right."

She dragged herself to a standing position and, with considerable effort, kept her voice reasonable. "Cash. I'll be fine. Believe me. But you have to let it go. You have to let *me* go."

The tension was back, in his shoulders and around his

eyes. "Damn it, Abby. You're as good as family to me. We had plans."

"Plans change."

"What does that mean? Are you talking forever? Are you saying you'll never come home?"

She wanted to drop back to the bed, burrow beneath the rumpled covers—and never come out. "Look, Cash. I don't know. Just, please, let me be for now."

But he refused to hear her. "Put on some clothes. We'll go eat."

She regarded him, shaking her head, absolutely certain that she could not face a plate of eggs at any time in the near future.

Still, if it was the only way to get rid of him…

"Breakfast," she bargained. "That's all. You'll say whatever else you think you have to say to me. And then you'll go home."

"I said I'm staying awhile."

She gave him her hardest look. "And I said you're not. Breakfast. And then you go."

He glared at her, but couldn't keep it up for long. He hung his head. "You hate me." He looked absolutely desolate.

Though he was fifteen years her senior, right at that moment, she felt a thousand years older than he would ever be. "No. I do not hate you. I could never hate you. But I need to be away from you, and…everything I grew up with, for a while. Until I figure things out. Nothing's…the way it used to be. And I'm having some trouble dealing with that."

She watched the deep sadness that clouded his eyes, a sadness that matched her own. "Ty," he said with quiet regret.

She nodded. Abby's father, Ty Heller, had been top

hand at the Bravo family's ranch for almost thirty years. Two months ago, he had rolled his ancient pickup down a ravine and broken his neck. Abby still had trouble believing that he was really gone.

Cash took a step toward her. "Abby..."

"Don't." She threw out a hand to ward him off.

He stopped, though his eyes pleaded with her. It had been the night of Ty's funeral when Cash had come to her, to offer comfort. To be comforted himself....

"Try to understand." Her voice was hardly more than a whisper. "I need some time here in Denver. On my own."

"Abby..."

"Let me go, Cash."

She saw the change in him as he accepted her will. He had a young man's face as a rule; a boyish look about him that women loved. But right then, he looked older than his thirty-six years.

"All right," he said flatly. "Breakfast. We'll talk a little more. Then, if you still want me to, I'll go."

At a coffee shop a few blocks from Abby's apartment, Cash ordered a western omelette and a stack of pancakes.

"I'll have a bran muffin," Abby said.

Cash took her menu from her. "You need eggs." He aimed one of his knock-'em-dead smiles at the waitress. "She'll have eggs. Scrambled. With sausage. Hash browns, sourdough toast and—"

"Cash."

"—a large milk."

"Just tea and the muffin," Abby said to the waitress.

The waitress looked at her patiently. "But, honey, he thinks you should have—"

"Tea and a muffin," she repeated through clenched teeth.

Cash said, "You'll want those eggs the minute you get them."

"For the last time. Tea. A muffin. That's all."

The waitress looked at Cash, a rueful, "what shall I do now, master?" sort of look. What was it about the man? All he had to do was smile at women, and they forgot that they had the right to vote now.

"It's my breakfast," Abby insisted.

"You need protein," Cash said.

She slapped her palm on the table. "Stop."

He widened those baby blues. "Stop what?"

"I can order my own food. You back off. I am not kidding."

For a suspended moment, they stared at each other, eye to eye and will to will. And then, elaborately, he shrugged. "You want to starve yourself I guess that's your business."

"You bet it's my business."

He turned a sheepish smile on the waitress. "Sorry, ma'am. I guess she just wants that muffin after all."

"Oh, it's no problem. Really. Is that all, then?"

"Yeah, I think that'll do it." He glanced at her name tag and then zapped her with another smile. "Betty."

Blushing prettily, Betty finished scribbling the order. Then she trotted away to do her master's bidding.

They got their food quickly, which was par for the course with Cash. He had a talent for making others want to please him. Women—and men, too—seemed to fall all over themselves seeing that his needs were met. And really, Abby thought, it didn't surprise her that people responded to him. He was generous and kind. And he gave others the feeling that he really *saw* them and cared about them.

He dug right in when Betty set his plate before him. Abby ignored her muffin and watched him, feeling fond in spite of herself, thinking how handsome and healthy and fine he was, even after a night spent drinking too much. A gorgeous man, all the way around.

He looked up from his plate to catch her watching him. She instantly dropped her gaze to her untouched muffin.

"You eat that," he commanded. She picked it up and began peeling off the paper muffin cup. She had popped a bite into her mouth and was chewing obediently, when he asked, "You will come home and see your mom before school starts again, won't you?"

She sipped tea, stalling, wishing he'd asked just about anything else but that. Abby loved her mother, but the two of them rarely saw eye to eye on anything. It had been Ty who understood her. And she didn't even want to think about what would happen when Edna Delacourt Heller learned about the baby.

So she *wouldn't* think about it. Not for a while yet, at least. And as far as the fall semester at C.U. went, well, she doubted she'd even be going. Right now, she needed to earn and save money. To that end, she was working two jobs. She served cocktails all night, which Cash had discovered. What he didn't know was that from nine to three, Monday through Friday, she waited tables at a coffee shop much like the one they sat in right now. She spent what spare time she had in search of bookkeeping work, which she prayed she would find before she got too big to be on her feet day and night.

Cash was watching her, waiting for an answer. "Well?"

She broke off another piece of muffin. "I'll try to get home for a visit as soon as I can."

He made a sound in his throat, an impatient sound. "Your mom needs to see you. You're all the family she's got now. And she's still grieving, with your dad gone."

"I said I'll try, Cash."

He dropped his fork, hard enough that it clattered against his plate. "Just say when you're coming. I'll make arrangements *not* to be around. How's that?"

"Stop." She aimed a look at him, a look as fierce and fiery as she could make it.

Carefully, he picked up his fork and finished his omelette.

Half an hour later, they arrived back at her apartment. She tried to tell him goodbye at the door, but he refused to take a hint. He pushed past her and gained the sanctuary of her room.

"One more thing," he announced, as he felt for the inside pocket of his western-cut suede jacket.

She knew what was coming. "Do not get out that checkbook."

He ignored her. He went over to the table, pulled out his platinum Cross pen and scribbled out a check. "Quit working at that bar." He ripped the check from the book and held it out to her. "This should hold you over until you can find something worth your while."

She remained at the door, her hands behind her back. "I can manage on my own."

"I'll just leave it right here."

"No."

Shaking his head, he put the check on the table. Then he slid the checkbook back to his pocket and put his pen away. "Well, I guess there's nothing more to—"

Before he could get the rest out, she marched over,

picked up the check and tore it in half, then tore the halves in half. After that, she threw the pieces in the air. Together, they watched them drift to the carpet at their feet.

He looked down at the torn remnants of his generosity. "What the hell good is that supposed to do?"

"What part of *no* was unclear to you?"

He pushed back the sides of his jacket and braced his hands on his lean hips. "This is stupid. Pointless. I've always helped you before. I've paid for half of your education, and you were never too proud to let me."

"Things were different then. You were investing in me. The more I learned in college, the more use I was to you."

"And now you're not?" He loomed closer, his voice rising in volume with his frustration. "What are you telling me? Are you saying that you're never coming back to work for me because I blew it and took you to bed?"

"Quiet down."

"Then answer me."

"All right. I'm saying I don't know. I'm saying I need time. I've *been* saying that all morning. But you're a pigheaded man. And you just aren't hearing."

"You're never going to forgive me, are you?"

"It's not a matter for forgiveness."

"That's what you say."

"Because it's true."

He took a step closer, so he was looming above her. "Then if you don't have to forgive me, why won't you—"

She cut him off. "I mean it, Cash. I am not coming home. You just have to let me be for a while."

"Abby, you have to listen. You have to see—"

"No." She tried to back away.

"Don't—" He reached out and grabbed her, his big hands closing on her upper arms.

She froze, sucking in a shocked gasp.

"Abby…" The word was an agony. And also a caress.

For a moment, she forgot how to breathe. Images of that night in April flashed through her mind.

Sorrow; he had looked at her with such sorrow. Sorrow for Ty, who had been like a father to him, and sorrow for her, too. In Cash's eyes that night she had seen all the sadness of the world. At first. But then, as she watched, that sorrow had changed to something else altogether.

She had felt as if her heart were lifting, rising to meet the look in his eyes. She had surged up, to press her open lips against his neck—to taste him with her tongue. He had made a sound then, an urgent, hungry sound. And reached for her. His mouth had covered hers, hot and consuming, tasting slightly of whiskey and the cigarettes he kept swearing he was going to give up.

After that first burning kiss, he had pulled away, looked down at her. His warm breath came ragged against her face. "Abby?" A question. A plea.

"Cash," she had answered, and dragged his head back down so that his lips could meet hers once more.

Abby closed her eyes, shutting out the sight of him now—and the memories of him then. Very gently, Cash released her.

"See?" she whispered, making herself look up at him again. "It can never be the same."

He stepped back, away from her. "You find a way to see your mom," he commanded harshly. "She hasn't been herself since your dad died. She needs you." And then he turned and went out the door.

Chapter Two

Cash flew his little Cessna four-seater out of Denver into Sheridan. From there, he got in his Cadillac and headed for home, which was Medicine Creek, a town with a population that hovered just below the thousand mark, not far from the eastern slopes of the Big Horn Mountains in northern Wyoming.

Medicine Creek looked like any number of small towns in the West. Its Main Street consisted primarily of flat-roofed buildings made of brick. The buildings housed bookstores and gift shops, a couple of diners and a couple of pricier restaurants. There was a new library, with floor-to-ceiling windows in front and a pretty good selection of books inside. There was the Oriental Hotel, which the Medicine Creek Historical Society had succeeded in having declared a historical building a few years before; both Teddy Roosevelt and the Sundance Kid had slept there—Sundance reputedly with his lady love, Emma Pace.

Cash lived in a big house of slate and brick on North Street. It was a nice, quiet street lined with cottonwood trees. He'd had the house built to his own specifications a decade earlier. As a rule, he enjoyed the large, airy rooms and vaulted ceilings. He was a man who liked lots of space. But that day, the damn big rooms seemed to echo. The house felt too empty.

He picked up the phone and called the ranch. Edna answered on the third ring.

"Rising Sun Ranch."

She sounded tired, he thought. He knew her so well. She'd treated him like her own when he'd come to live with his grandparents all those years ago; a ten-year-old boy who'd needed someone to mother him, though nothing would have made him admit it at the time.

"Edna?"

He knew she was smiling even before she said his name.

"Cash. I was hoping we'd hear from you today."

He also knew she was hoping he'd have something good to tell her about Abby.

So much for Edna's hopes.

"What's for dinner?" he asked.

"Oh, roast chicken. Oven-browned potatoes. Snap beans with bacon. Fresh-baked bread, gelatin mold salad...."

"I'll be there in an hour."

They sat down to eat around seven. There were just three of them: Edna, Cash and Zach, Cash's cousin. Zach Bravo had been running the Rising Sun since their grandfather, Ross Bravo, had died five years before.

The table seemed even bigger than usual, with only the three of them. But Edna liked to eat there. She'd assumed the role of hostess at Bravo family events almost a quarter of a century before, after Cash's grandmother, Matty, passed away. Then, five years ago, after Ross had been laid to rest beside Matty, Zach had invited the Hellers to move out of the foreman's cottage across the yard and into the main house. Edna had quickly agreed.

But even before the Hellers actually moved in, it had always seemed to Cash as if the house belonged as much to them as it did to the Bravos. Edna kept the rooms smelling of lemon wax; she hummed in the kitchen while she cooked for the family and the hands. Ty used to sit out on the wide front porch of an evening, his boots up on the porch rail—a man who felt himself at home. And whenever Cash came out from town, they all ate together, as a family: Zach, Cash, Ty, Edna—and Ross, before his death. Nate, too, whenever he showed up for a visit. And Abby...

It caused a tightness in Cash's chest to think of her. But he couldn't help himself, sitting here at this table, where she'd eaten pretty much all of her dinners for the first eighteen years of her life.

Abby had been born at the ranch, over in the foreman's cottage, during a spring blizzard when there'd been no way for Edna to make it to the hospital in Buffalo. Cash had been scared to death for Edna, since his own mother had died in childbirth. But Edna had lived. And produced the miracle of Abby. They hadn't let him in the cottage during the birth. But not long after, as soon as mother and child had been cleaned up, Ty had come out and found him skulking around the front door, scared to death of what might be happening inside.

"Get your butt on in here, boy," Ty had commanded. Inside, Ty had let him hold Abby, so tiny and red faced.

Right now, it seemed to him that he had sat at this table and watched her grow up. He could see her as if she really were there across from him, at about three years old—the age when Edna had declared her ready to eat with the big folks. She'd thrown a handful of boiled carrots across the table and been sent to her room in disgrace.

He recalled her at six—or was it seven?—wearing jeans and a T-shirt, her mouth set in a mutinous line— just before Edna sent her away again, because she had dirt under her nails and Edna wouldn't stand for that. And at eleven, all dressed up for some reason in a pretty blue dress. And at fifteen, when he'd noticed she was wearing eye makeup. Cash had frowned at her, wondering why she thought she needed to wear makeup. She had stuck out her tongue at him. And by then she'd been smart enough to wait until Edna couldn't see.

"So how's Abby doing down there in Denver?" Zach asked into the silence that had settled over the table. Zach was like that; sometimes they all wondered if he thought of anything but cows and bulls and the land he loved more than the average man could love a woman. But then he'd open his mouth and out would come exactly what everyone else was wondering about—but didn't have the nerve to mention.

Cash shot a glance at Edna. She seemed composed, though she'd set down her fork and her smile looked pinched at the corners.

"Yes," Edna said, sounding too polite. "How *is* Abigail?"

Cash recalled dark circles under hazel eyes and a fleabag one-room apartment strewn with clothes and books. "She seemed...okay."

Edna waited, still smiling her pinched smile at him. Zach waited, too, watching Cash, wearing one of those completely unreadable Zach-like looks.

"What?" Cash said, as if he didn't know.

"'Okay' doesn't tell us a hell of a lot," Zach said dryly.

"All right." Cash had the urge to loosen his collar, a stupid urge, since his shirt was already open at the neck. "I'm getting to it."

They went on watching him.

"She's working a lot. She's real busy. She seemed...tired."

"Where is she working?" Edna asked.

"Mac's Mile High, I think it's called."

"Mac's Mile High what?"

He coughed. "Saloon. Mac's Mile High Saloon."

"A bar." Edna put her slender, work-chapped hand over her heart. "Why is she doing this? What has come over her?"

Her father's dead. And on the night of the day that they put him in the ground, I took her virginity out in the barn, Cash thought. That's why she's doing this. That's what's come over her.

"She should be here, at home," Edna said. "Working for you. The way she's always done since she was sixteen."

Cash said nothing; he just sat there, despising himself.

"That's what I really don't understand," Edna went on. "Of course, we all know that Abigail and I have our differences. And I can almost understand that she might want to take off on her own for a time, after...losing Ty. But that she'd do this to you, Cash. That she'd not show up to handle your office, when you were counting on her. After all you've done for her, it just doesn't—''

Cash couldn't take any more. ''Edna. The office isn't a big deal.''

''Oh, you say that, but still—''

''I mean it. It's nothing. I hardly use it anyway. It's just an address to put on my letterhead. And Renata is there. She can handle the phones and the mail.''

''It's not the phones. Or the mail. And I know that *you* are the heart of Cash Ventures, Incorporated, that it's your charm and your willingness to take a chance, not to mention your good sense for a strong investment, that makes you a successful man. But I also know how you and Abby are. Always with your heads together, always making plans. And she *has* become quite useful to you, since she's learned so much about number cracking and all.''

''Number crunching.''

''Yes. Exactly. Did you tell her to call me?''

Had he? In so many words? He couldn't exactly remember.

''You didn't tell her to call me?''

The hurt in her eyes, hazel eyes like Abby's, broke his heart.

''Cash?''

''I...told her to get home to see you, as soon as possible.''

''Did she say that she would?''

He couldn't bear to give her the truth. So he didn't. ''Uh, yeah. She did. You know she did.''

''Oh, I don't understand.'' Edna shook her head. ''I just don't understand. She could at least return my calls.''

Zach spoke softly. ''She's twenty-one. A grown-up. Maybe we have to let her do things her own way now.''

Edna pressed her lips together, collecting herself. And then she gave Zach a brave smile. "Yes. I know, I know." She turned her smile on Cash. "Thank you. For going. For checking to see that she's all right."

"Damn it, don't thank me!" The words exploded out of him, harsh and angry, full of all the frustration he was trying so hard to control.

Edna's smile wavered. "Cash?"

He sucked in a long gulp of air. "I'm sorry. I'm...a little on the edgy side, I guess."

Edna nodded sadly. "Yes, I know. I understand."

There was a long, heavy silence, which Zach ended by asking, "Was that apple pie I saw on the kitchen counter?"

Edna put on her brave smile again. "It certainly was." She pushed back her chair and stood. And then, for a moment, she wavered and leaned on the table.

Both Zach and Cash jumped to their feet.

"Edna?" Zach asked. "You all right?"

She pushed away from the table and smoothed her hair with a shaky hand. "Fine."

"You look pale," Cash said. "Maybe we should—"

"I said I'm fine. I simply stood up too fast, that's all."

"But—"

"No buts. Both of you sit down." She was already in motion, gathering up their empty plates. "I'll just go and see about fresh coffee and that pie."

Cash stayed after dinner to go over the accounts with Zach.

The ranch, which covered roughly a hundred square miles and was home to around twelve hundred head of cattle, belonged jointly to the three Bravo cousins: Cash, Zach and Nate. But in an era when beef prices never went high enough and one drought seemed to follow another, it was Zach who made the Rising Sun Cattle Company a going concern. For years now, both Cash and Nate had pretty much gone their own ways. Neither of them would have minded at all if Zach just took care of the place and let them show up when the urge struck—or gave them a call when he turned up shorthanded during calving season or at branding time.

But Zach took his stewardship seriously. So whenever Cash or Nate came out to the ranch, they always seemed to end up crowded around Zach's computer, staring at columns of numbers that proved Zach was doing one hell of a job.

By the time they finished that night, eleven o'clock had come and gone. Cash decided against driving back to town.

"You know your room is always ready for you," Edna told him fondly. Though it had long ago been done over into a guest room, Edna still called it *his* room. She always put him there whenever he stayed the night.

Unfortunately, he'd forgotten that he could see the barn from the window of that room. So instead of going to bed, he ended up standing in the dark, looking out at the silvery light of the full moon reflected off the barn walls.

And remembering what he had no right to remember...

Hearing again the sound of Abby's sobs, which had led him to her, in one of the vacant stalls. Smelling the humid, pungent odors of hay and animals. Feeling once more the sudden, shocking, incredible caress of Abby's mouth against his throat; her sweet, ragged breath across his skin. Seeing the absolute trust in her eyes when he looked down at her—and covered her mouth with his own....

With a low oath, Cash turned away from the window. He threw himself on the bed fully clothed, not even bothering to pull off his boots. He ached for a cigarette. Just one.

But he'd given them up again, this morning, after smoking a whole pack in the bar of his Denver hotel last night.

He closed his eyes. He started counting oil wells, which was his own private joke on himself. His daddy, Johnny Bravo, had made it big on an oil well that came in a gusher down in Carbon County. Cash had invested in an oil well or two himself in his time. So when he couldn't sleep, he didn't count sheep. He counted oil wells.

Somewhere around three or four thousand, he must have dropped off.

He dreamed of things he had no right to dream of. Later, he awoke and found himself staring at the ceiling, remembering those dreams, hard as some randy kid. He lay there, hating himself some more, not only for what he'd done but for the fact that remembering what he'd done had the power to arouse him. On top of hating himself, he tried to figure out what in the hell he could do to make things right again.

He couldn't come up with a damn thing. And he couldn't get back to sleep, either. He glanced at the clock on the bedstand to his right. It was nearing 5 a.m. He'd slept longer than he'd thought. Soon Zach would be up. A rancher to his bones, Zacharius Bravo. He never took a vacation and rarely gave himself a day off. Three hundred sixty-five days a year, he was up before dawn, whether there was any reason to be up at that godforsaken hour or not.

Edna would be up shortly, too, banging those pots and

pans, getting breakfast ready for Zach and the three hands out in the trailers next to the foreman's cottage. If Cash wanted to sleep in, she'd always fix him something special later on.

Well, this was one day when he wouldn't put Edna out. He swung his boots to the floor and sat up with a groan. He raked his hair back with his hands. As he rubbed his gritty-feeling eyes, it occurred to him that he should probably hit the shower. But he wanted coffee first.

Downstairs, he stood for a minute in the doorway to the kitchen. Edna was there, at the table bent over some papers. He waited for her to look up and see him.

And when she did, he had to stifle a gasp. Her face had a bluish cast and the skin around her lips was dead white.

"God. Edna…"

She smiled, a death's-head grin, and gamely held up a pen. "I was trying to write to her. I thought maybe a letter would make her see—"

"Edna, what the hell is wrong with you?"

She waved the pen, as if his question meant nothing. "I just want her home. I want to see her. I need to see her. Sometimes I wake up in the morning and I wonder if there's anyone left for me. Without Ty. Without my little girl…"

"Edna, *what is wrong?*"

For a moment, she kept smiling that scary smile, and then she frowned. "I don't know. I've been up all night." She put a fist against her chest. "This crushing pain. Like someone dropped a boulder on me, right here. All night long."

He was already at the phone, dialing 911.

"I kept thinking it would go away," he heard Edna murmuring as he waited for someone to pick up the damn phone on the other end. "I didn't want to wake you or Zach. You boys need your sleep...."

Chapter Three

"We should call Abby," Zach said hours later.

Cash and his cousin sat in the small waiting room of the hospital in Buffalo. The doctor had just been out to explain to them that it looked as if Edna had had a heart attack—but they couldn't be sure yet. Half of her heart had stopped working, the doctor had said, but they were confused about her blood test results. A helicopter would take her to the big hospital in Billings right away, where they would learn more.

"Do you want me to do it?" Zach asked.

Cash blinked and tried to stop worrying about Edna. "What?"

Zach sighed. "Do you want me to call Abby?"

"What for?"

"Because she should know."

Cash stared at his cousin. Then he nodded. "You're right. And she should be here." He stood. "I'll go get her. Right now. Can you hold down the fort on this end?"

"Hell, Cash."

"What? You know she'll get to Billings one way or another. Might as well fly her myself."

"Yeah, but…"

Cash saw something in Zach's eyes he wasn't sure he liked. All at once, he wondered how much his cousin knew. "But what?"

"Maybe she'd like a little warning."

"Warning? What for? She doesn't need a warning. She needs to be with her mother."

Zach shook his head.

"What?" Cash demanded again. "You got something on your mind, you better say it."

Zach shrugged. "No, you're right. She'll want to be with Edna, pronto. So go get her."

One by one, Abby set three longnecks in front of three thirsty urban cowboys, then she scooped up the icy mugs from her tray and plunked them in the middle of the table. "Enjoy."

"Thank you, ma'am." The tallest of the three customers pushed back his white Stetson and tossed some bills on her tray.

"I'll be right back with your change."

"You keep that."

Abby murmured her thanks and turned for the bar. She got about two steps before she saw Cash standing over by the door, scanning the club and looking break-your-heart handsome.

Her mouth went dry and her pulse went crazy. Before she could move another inch, he saw her. She felt pinned to the spot by those eyes of his.

But she didn't stay pinned. She marched to the bar, set down her tray and muttered to Mac, the bartender and owner, "I need a break."

Mac, who saw everything, was looking at Cash. "Ten minutes. No more."

"No problem," she said, with more assurance than she felt.

She approached Cash. "This way." She led him through a side door to another room furnished much like the main bar, with small round tables and bentwood chairs. Mac called it the party room and rented it out to groups.

Abby flicked a wall switch. The overhead lights came on, harsh and much brighter than the dim lights in the main bar behind her. She closed the door and gestured at a chair. Cash dropped into it.

She looked at him in the brighter light—and felt the first stab of alarm. Until that moment, she'd imagined it was just going to be more of the same: he demanding she come home and she insisting that she wouldn't.

But something else was going on. He was too quiet. He looked exhausted. And the shadow of worry in his eyes seemed so deep, so very dark.

"What is it? What's happened?"

He closed his eyes. "Abby..."

She sat in the chair opposite him, leaned across the table and put her hand over his. He stiffened, and then he turned his hand, enclosing hers. At that moment, they were what they had once been: Cash and Abby. Comrades. Family.

"Tell me," she said, willing strength into his hand, drawing strength from him at the same time.

"It's Edna...."

"God." The single word was a prayer. She squeezed Cash's hand, and felt him squeeze back.

"Something's happened," he said. "They think a heart attack, but they're not sure yet."

"She's...?" Somehow Abby couldn't make herself say the word *dead*.

Cash hastened to reassure her. "She's alive. I swear to you. I called Zach just a few minutes ago, before I came in here, so I could tell you for certain. They say she's stabilized. But something's wrong. Only half of her heart is working."

"Where is she?"

"They took her to Buffalo first, and then put her in a helicopter and flew her to Billings."

"You flew your own plane here?"

"Yeah."

"You'll take me to her?"

"You know I will."

She pulled her hand from Cash's grip and pushed back her chair. "Let's go."

Mac muttered a few choice epithets when Abby said she had to go. But then he wished her Godspeed and called his wife, Millie, to come in and finish out Abby's shift.

Abby returned to her apartment just long enough to throw some things in a suitcase. She didn't have time to think about the recently sensitive state of her stomach until she was strapped into one of the seats in Cash's little plane. But she needn't have worried. She'd never been sick before in small planes, and she wasn't this time, either.

It was nearly dawn by the time they got to Billings.

Cash had a rental car waiting. He drove them straight to the hospital.

They found Zach in the little waiting room outside the intensive care unit. He stood when he saw them. Abby rushed to him, and he enfolded her in his arms.

"Good to see you, Pint-Size," he whispered in her ear.

She held on tight. "Same back to you."

Zach was actually younger than Cash by a couple of years. But to Abby, he always seemed older, so mature and settled down. He possessed a deep calm that never failed to soothe her.

She stepped away and mustered up a smile. "So. How is she doing?"

Briefly, he brought them up to date. The doctors had run more tests. Evidently, a certain enzyme always showed up in the blood when a heart attack had taken place. Edna's bloodstream had no trace of it. Still, half of her heart wasn't functioning. So they'd gone in through an artery in her thigh and inserted a device that would help her heart to beat regularly until they could figure out what the hell was going on.

"She has to lie completely still," Zach said, "so they've got her pretty doped up."

"Can I see her?"

"Come on." He led them through a pair of swinging doors and past a large central nurses' station. He waved at a nurse and she gave him a nod, so he moved on to one of the rooms.

In the room, Edna lay faceup on a metal-railed bed. Tubes seemed to be everywhere: they emerged from the back of one hand, the crook of an elbow and also from the sheet that covered her thin chest. Around her were way too many machines and monitors, each one ticking or bubbling or beeping or making strange breathing sounds.

Cash and Zach hung back as Abby walked around the far side of the bed. At the metal railing there, careful of all the tubes and machines, she stood looking down at her mother.

Edna's eyes were closed. Her eyelids looked paper-thin and bluish. And her face looked…so old. Her hair was all smashed down, too. Abby hated seeing her like that. Because she knew how her mother would hate looking like that. Edna always took care to keep herself neat and tidy. And she wore a little mascara and lipstick, too, as a rule—applied with a very light hand, of course.

The paper-thin eyelids fluttered open. "Abigail." There was such relief on that old-looking face. "You've come."

"Mom." She wanted to touch the thin hand, but she feared she might disturb all the tubes stuck in the back of it. "How are you doing?"

"I've been better."

Abby nodded in understanding.

"I must remain very still. But it's not hard, with whatever it is they've been giving me. So tired.…" Her eyelids fluttered down again.

Abby didn't move. She watched her mother sleep, thinking of all the battles they'd fought with each other over the years. Sometimes Edna drove her crazy. But still, there was love between them. Right then, Abby felt that love as a physical force, deep, fierce and true. Death might have snatched away her father, but death could not have her mother. Not for years yet. Abby wouldn't let it.

Edna opened her eyes again. "You'll come home now?" she asked in a thin, plaintive voice.

It was blackmail, pure and simple. Emotional blackmail. And Abby knew it.

She thought of the baby growing inside her, but instead of feeling overwhelmed as she had for so many weeks now, she felt energized. It came to her: she wanted the baby, *really* wanted it, with no doubts and no ambivalence. She had never been a girl who'd played with dolls, who'd dreamed of a husband, babies and a home to keep. But now, at last, she truly understood that she would be a mother, like her own mother. And that she would give herself heart and soul to the task.

"Abigail?"

She thought of Cash, not ten feet away, watching. All she had to do was turn her head to see him. It had finally become real to her: he would have to know. Somehow, she would have to tell him.

And he would want to take over. He'd insist on marriage. At first.

But she would just have to be strong enough and sure enough of herself that she could tell him no and mean it. She wouldn't marry any man just because they had made a baby together; he'd have to accept that. They'd learn to work together to raise their child, with respect for each other as independent adults.

"Abigail." Edna's reedy voice was petulant now. "Will you come home?"

Abby smiled at her mother. "Hush. Settle down. You know I will."

Except to go to the bathroom and grab a few bites in the cafeteria, Abby refused to leave her mother's side through that entire day. Finally, around seven that night, after a lengthy consultation with a doctor who insisted that Edna would not expire if Abby took a break, Cash convinced her to check into a hotel.

But she would only stay there long enough to shower and change. And then she made him drive her back to the hospital.

"Now," she told Cash and Zach, "I want you both to get out of here. Get a good dinner and get some sleep."

They tried to argue, but she held firm. At last, they gave in and left. The ICU nurses, seeing how tired she looked, took pity on her and had a bed rolled into her mother's room. She fell into it gratefully and closed her eyes.

"Abigail?"

Her mother's voice sought her out through the darkness and the beeping and bubbling of all those lifesaving machines.

"Umm?"

"Thank you."

"What for?"

"You know."

Abby smiled to herself. "I'm here. I'm not going anywhere."

"Exactly."

"Good night, Mom."

Instead of saying good-night, Edna murmured dreamily, "Your father always promised me my own house, did you know that?"

Abby opened her eyes and stared into the darkness. She didn't speak.

Edna went on anyway. "But I never got my house. We never had that kind of money. So I spent our life together taking care of the Bravo house. And I didn't mind it, really. Not most of the time. Those boys needed me. They're like my own…but not really my own.''

Edna fell silent. For a moment, Abby thought she had dropped off to sleep again.

But then she said, ''Abby? Are you still awake?''

''Yes, Mom.''

''I'm fortunate, I know. I've managed to save some. And we did have a little life insurance, because I insisted. So I won't be destitute when I can't work anymore.'' She made a low sound, perhaps a chuckle. ''Zach. Mr. Responsible. He's seen I have good health insurance, so this episode will all be taken care of.''

''Good.''

''But we both know Cash would take care of me anyway, even if there was no savings and no insurance at all.''

''Yes. He would.''

''And Nate would come all the way from L.A. if necessary, to help me.'' Edna made that sound again, that sound that might have been a chuckle. ''Your father. Like the wind. Who can tie down the wind?''

''No one.''

''I did love him. I don't think I knew…how much. Until he was gone.''

''Mom…''

''I loved him.'' She sounded almost defiant. ''And I love you.''

''I know you do, Mom.''

''So very much.…''

''Go to sleep now.''

Edna sighed and said no more.

Abby lay in the darkness, listening to the machines for a while. Soon enough, exhaustion claimed her.

She awoke in the middle of the night when a nurse

came in to check on Edna. And she felt her stomach rise and roll.

Stifling a groan, she slid from the bed. Luckily, the bathroom was only a few feet away. She pushed the door closed and got her head over the toilet basin before the scanty contents of her stomach came up. She tried to be as quiet as she could.

When the retching finally stopped, she turned on the light and held back another groan at the sight of herself in the medicine cabinet mirror.

"So attractive," she whispered to her own haggard image.

She cleaned up as best she could. Then she turned off the light and waited for her eyes to become accustomed to the gloom.

Slowly, quietly, she pulled open the door. The room beyond was quiet, except for the machines. The nurse had gone. She tiptoed to the bed and looked down at her mother.

Sound asleep.

Abby went back to her own bed and slid beneath the sheet. Within minutes, dreams embraced her.

It was a week before Edna left the hospital. Zach went back to the ranch the day after Abby arrived. The next day, Cash got a call from one of his business associates about a land deal they were working on. Abby told him to go handle it; she could look after her mother just fine on her own. She felt relief when he agreed to go, because sometimes, when he looked at her, she was sure he knew her secret—which she did intend to tell him about.

Soon. Very soon.

Before he left, Cash made sure she had a rental car so that she could get around.

The doctors ran more tests. Finally, they told Abby that Edna had experienced a coronary vasospasm, and not a real heart attack.

"A coronary vasospasm," the doctor said, "amounts to severe, extended cramping of the heart muscle. It is not a heart attack—there is no disease involved. It's like a big charley horse. But it's dangerous because it's happening to the heart."

They couldn't say why it had happened. But they did say that Edna's arteries were surprisingly clear, with very little plaque buildup. Thus, with time, she would probably recover completely. Of course, she'd have to take it nice and easy for a while. And for the rest of her life, she would require medication to keep the problem from recurring.

Cash returned on Sunday, a week after Edna became ill. By then, they had taken her off the device that helped her heart to pump and moved her from intensive care into a regular room.

He appeared in the afternoon, while Edna was napping and Abby sat in a chair in the corner playing Super MarioKart on a Game Boy that one of the nurses had lent her. She was so intent on trying to pass Yoshi without spinning off the track that she didn't know Cash had come in until he spoke.

"Are you winning?"

Her nimble thumbs went slack. Mario whirled off into oblivion. She looked up. "I was."

Those gorgeous blue eyes scanned her face.

"You look better. More rested."

Her foolish heart trip-hammered against her breastbone. She prayed he couldn't hear it. "Not a lot to do around here *but* rest."

He went on looking at her. And she looked back.

Then he seemed to shake himself. "How is she?"

"I'm right here, Cash Bravo," Edna said. "Turn around and see for yourself."

He did turn. "Well, well," he said. "Beautiful. Downright beautiful."

Edna was blushing. Abby thought she really did look pretty, in a new bed jacket, with her hair neatly combed—and just a touch of blusher and lipstick.

"You look like you're ready to go home," Cash said, taking her hand.

"They said I could. Tomorrow."

For a moment, he just held Edna's hand.

Then she asked, "Are you staying the night here in Billings?"

"You bet."

"Then would you do a favor?"

"Name it."

"I want you to take Abigail out for dinner."

Panic lanced through Abby. Of course she needed to tell Cash her secret. But she wasn't quite ready yet. And until she *was* ready, she wanted to avoid spending time alone with him. She jumped to her feet. "No, really. I'd rather—"

Edna didn't let her finish. "Nonsense. All you do is sit here with me. And I'm getting along just fine now. A nice dinner out will be good for you."

"Mom…"

"Cash. Will you do that for me?"

They went to a steak house.

Abby's stomach had been behaving much better in the past few days, probably a result of the extra rest she was getting. Confident she could handle a nice, juicy porterhouse, she ordered one, along with a salad and a baked potato smothered in sour cream and chives.

"And hot tea." She smiled at the waitress.

As soon as the waitress had walked away, Cash demanded, "What's this tea you're always drinking lately?"

It occurred to her that he'd given her the perfect opening. She should tell him the truth right now. But she just wasn't ready yet. "I like tea. So what?"

He took a sip of the drink the waitress had brought him earlier, then shrugged. "I don't know. I just wondered."

She felt defensive—because she knew that she was going to sit across from him through the entire meal and not say a word about something that would change both their lives irrevocably. "If I want tea, I'll have tea."

"Abby, come on."

She glanced away, knowing herself to be petulant and cowardly—and not liking herself much at all. "I'm sorry." She met his eyes.

He looked back at her in a way that made her more uncomfortable than ever.

"I know you didn't want to come out to eat with me. And believe me, I understand your feelings."

No, you don't, she wanted to say. You don't understand at all. Because I can't seem to tell you. I can't *stand* to tell you....

"Abby, we're going to have learn to get along. We're going to have to get past what happened."

She swallowed. "I know."

The waitress came with their salads. For a few blessed minutes, Abby concentrated on forking up lettuce leaves and putting them in her mouth.

Cash sipped his drink again. "I'd like to just...let it

go. Forget it ever happened. If you could do that. Could you?''

She almost dared to answer, Well, that might be kind of difficult, considering I'm pregnant. But she didn't dare. She didn't say a word, only looked at him.

He set down his drink. ''Okay, stupid suggestion.''

She put down her fork. ''Look. Can we just eat, please? Can we just…not talk about it? I mean it, Cash. If every time I'm with you, we have to rehash it all again, I, well, I think I'll go plain crazy, you know?''

''Yeah. Fine. I get the message.'' He picked up a piece of bread and tore it in half.

They finished their salads and the waitress brought the main course. Abby cut off a bite of her porterhouse. It was delicious. But her appetite had fled. Across from her, Cash looked miserable.

She forced herself to speak in a bright tone. ''Well, it seems like I'll be coming home for the summer after all.''

He kept watching her, broodingly. ''That's something, I guess.'' He raised his hand for the waitress.

She appeared from thin air, eager to serve him, as all waitresses were. ''What can I get you?''

He pointed at his drink.

''Coming right up.'' She bounced happily away.

Abby tried again to talk about everyday matters, to get them back on some kind of even ground with each other. ''I think as soon as we get Mom settled at home, I'll fly to Denver.''

He lifted a bronze eyebrow. ''Why?''

''Well, to get my things, to close up my apartment and to pick up my car.'' She had already called Mac and the manager of the coffee shop where she worked days and told them she wouldn't be returning.

''Forget that,'' Cash said.

For a moment, Abby thought he was talking to the waitress, who'd just reappeared with his fresh drink. But then he went on.

"I handled it."

Abby frowned. "You what?"

"I arranged to have your things sent home and told the manager at your apartment that you wouldn't need the place anymore. I also hired someone to drive your car home."

She stared at him.

He waved a hand. "Your mother needs you now. You can't be fooling around in Denver."

"That's not the point."

"It sure as hell is."

"They were *my* things, Cash. This is *my* life."

"You're making a big deal out of nothing."

"No, I'm not." She reached for her water glass and then set it down, hard enough that water sloshed on the tablecloth.

"Abby..."

"No." She leaned across the table and kept her voice to a whisper. "You can't take over my life, Cash. You can't fix everything for me. I'm twenty-one. It's time I fixed things for myself. Do you understand?"

He sat back and sighed. "You always used to let me do whatever I thought was best for you. You'd just say thanks and let it be."

He was right, so it took her a moment to compose a reply. When she spoke, she made her tone gentler than before. "I know. You've been good to me. But I really do want to make my own decisions now. And I want you to let me."

"You wouldn't be saying this if it wasn't for—"

She didn't let him finish. "Look. I've told you more

than once that I don't blame you for what happened. And I meant it. So just give up feeling guilty, why don't you?''

He looked sheepish—and so handsome it hurt.

"I'll try."

They managed to get through the rest of the meal without incident. He took her back to the hospital for a while after that. And then he returned her to her hotel, where he had a room, too.

She thought that maybe she'd gotten through to him, at least about trying to run her life for her—until the next morning, when she went to check out of her room and learned he'd already paid the bill. She spoke to him about that briefly, before they went to drop off her rental car and pick up Edna for the drive home.

"Cash, you can't just pay all my bills."

"Why not?"

She remained calm. "Because they're *my* bills."

"Are you coming back to work for me?"

"Cash…"

"You know it's the best thing. How do you expect me to keep track of my money, without you and all those damn spreadsheets of yours? And you won't find another job that pays as well—or that you can do at home, where you can keep an eye on Edna at the same time."

She was shaking her head.

He put on that boyish look that knocked all the women dead. "Come on. Work for me."

And she heard herself giving in, saying yes.

He grinned and told her he'd take the cost of the hotel room out of her paycheck, over time, if she insisted. And the same went for her rental car.

Abby told herself they'd come to some sort of understanding, that even though she'd agreed to work for him, which was bound to cause some problems, at least he would stop trying to take over her life. But then, when they went home, he drove to Medicine Creek instead of out to the ranch. He pulled onto Meadowlark Lane, a street a few blocks from his.

Abby saw her battered Rabbit right away, parked in the driveway of a neat two-story brick house with a big, spreading cottonwood tree in the front yard. Cash turned in and parked beside the Rabbit.

"What's this?" Edna asked, her eyes shining.

"I think it's about time you had your own house," Cash said.

Chapter Four

"Oh, Cash." Edna sounded young, full of life and joy. "I just...I can't believe it!"

Cash basked in her excitement. Over a year before, Ty had told him how much Edna longed for her own house.

That had been during the spring trail drive, which took place every April; Zach would get together whatever hands he had working for him, and a neighbor or two, and move a good half of the herd up to higher pastures for the warmer months. Cash had been helping out with the spring drive since the first year he'd come to live at the ranch. Some years, if they stopped at fenced land for the night, they'd go on home to sleep.

But last year, they'd taken a little different route and ended up spending one night on open land, in a camper trailer, watching over the herd. Early on, as the hands took a turn circling the herd, Cash and Ty sat out under the stars for a while, sharing a nip or two, talking about nothing in particular. Somewhere in the conversation, Ty had mentioned that he'd never bought Edna the house he'd always promised her.

"If there's anything I got regrets about, it's that," he'd said. Then he'd looked up at the shadows of the Big Horn Mountains, capped with their glittering mantle of snow, and lifted a thermos with whiskey-laced coffee in it. "Nothin' else. Nothin' else at all."

On the day Ty died, Cash had remembered what Ty had said that cold spring night under the stars. And he'd decided to see to it that Edna got her house.

What had happened after the funeral between him and Abby had nothing to do with his decision. Nothing at all.

He'd bought the house two weeks after Ty's death. It was just right. It had a master suite downstairs for Edna, and two spare rooms upstairs: one for Abby when she came home, and one, as it turned out, that Abby could use as an office. Escrow had closed without a hitch. But he'd wanted to fix it up nice before giving it to Edna, so he'd sort of back-burnered the project until he'd had a little spare time to finish it up right.

Edna's illness had motivated him. During her hospital stay, he'd overseen the delivery of two moving vans full of furniture in solid, conservative styles. Then he'd spent all day last Saturday moving the stuff into the rooms with the help of a couple of local kids. He'd even hired a woman to come in and put the new sheets on the beds, as well as to fill the kitchen cabinets with packaged goods.

"Oh, Cash." Edna hung on his arm as he gave her and Abby the tour. "How could you have known? It's exactly as I always dreamed it might be. Even the furniture...."

"I've seen you studying those JC Penney catalogs. I think, after all these years, I know what you like."

"I don't know what to say."

"Then don't say a thing." He glanced at Abby. Her face wore that closed, tight look it wore too much lately. He looked at Edna again, drank in her smile. "It's your retirement present—if you want to retire, I mean. You know you won't have to. Zach would be more than glad to have you back, when you're feeling better. But this house will always be here, waiting for you."

She gave his arm another squeeze. "I think I'll have to pinch myself. Is this really real?"

"You bet it is."

They walked slowly up the stairs, in consideration for Edna's weakened condition. He showed them the room that would be Abby's bedroom.

Abby pulled open the closet door. "Why, all my clothes are here," she sneered. "Already put away. Isn't that convenient?"

Cash just looked at her, feeling reproachful. He had only wanted to help.

"Abigail..." Edna murmured warningly.

Abby fell silent, but her eyes were mutinous.

And then, when she saw her computer and all her accounting software and books in the office room, she looked madder than a teased hornet.

"Thank you," she said in a tone that didn't sound grateful at all.

He just went ahead and smiled at her. "You're welcome. Renata will be expecting you over at the office tomorrow. You can pick up the books and things from her."

"Fine."

"I'll let you get them in order, and then I thought I'd drop by in a few days so we can go over everything."

"Great."

Edna patted his arm again. "Cash, I am just completely overwhelmed."

Abby muttered something too low to make out.

"What was that, Abigail?" Edna asked sharply.

"Nothing."

She stuck out her lip. Cash thought she looked just like the kid she constantly insisted she wasn't anymore.

Cash smiled at Edna. Her eyes sparkled with happiness. Still, she had to be careful not to wear herself out. The doctors had said she'd need a lot of rest, that she wasn't to do anything strenuous for at least the next month. "You should get yourself to bed."

"Yes. Of course. You're right."

He took her back down the stairs and saw her settled in the big reclining chair he'd bought for her, in the nice little sitting area of her bedroom where she could look out on the box elder tree that grew in the backyard. Then he went outside to bring in the two small suitcases in the trunk.

Abby had beaten him to it. She was trudging up the stairs when he got to the front hall.

"Abby."

She stopped at the top and looked down at him, her straw-colored hair falling in her eyes, her mouth set in a defiant line.

"I would have brought those in."

"Oh, I know you would."

He mounted the first step. "Abby…"

She just looked at him, daring him with those eyes of hers to take another step. She was breathing a little fast.

He could see her breasts, beneath the white shirt she wore, rising and falling.

He knew what those breasts looked like naked, what they felt like in his hands....

"What?" she said.

"Nothing." He turned before she could look down and see that he hadn't put that one night behind him—not by a long shot.

"Cash." Now she sounded sorry.

He froze, looking away from her, a few steps from the front door, not daring to turn back on the chance that she might see his shame. "Yeah?"

"She wanted a house...so bad. How did you know?" Her voice was soft.

"Ty told me. A year ago."

She was quiet for a moment, then she sighed. "I'm mad at you."

"I know."

"You will not run my life."

"You've said that."

"But...thank you. For her."

"Welcome," he muttered. And then he got the hell out.

Cash returned on Thursday. He visited with Edna, and then he and Abby retreated to her office.

Abby thought that he seemed edgy at first, once they were alone. He took pains to stay well away from her, on the far side of her desk. But she had decided that she would really put some effort into getting along with him. After all, they did have to work together.

And he *was* the father of her baby—which she intended to tell him about. As soon as she could reestablish some semblance of the old easiness between them.

She'd set a goal for that day: to get their working relationship back on track. To that end, she stayed cheerful and professional and never once hinted that she sensed any tension in the air.

She showed him how she'd started to pull his books back together and promised to have everything pretty much under control within a week or so. She smiled and sat back in her chair and asked him about his latest land deal.

He seemed to relax as he talked about it. They discussed grain futures and the encouraging rise in uranium prices.

Before he left, she brought up the subject of Josh DeMarley. Josh, an old high school buddy of Cash's, always had some oil well that was supposed to make him rich. But he never got rich. Between loans and "investments," Cash had passed a significant sum Josh's way over the years—money Cash would never see again.

Abby tried to sound stern. "I want you to promise me that the next time he comes to you with some crazy wildcatting scheme, you'll tell him no."

Cash looked at Abby reproachfully. "You know I can't promise anything like that. Josh and I go way back. He's got a wife and a little girl. And he's had bad luck."

"He *is* bad luck," Abby said.

"It's only money. And you know me. I can always make more."

That much was true. Money seemed to seek him out. It had been like that since he was a very small child.

He had earned the name Cash at the age of seven when his parents, Johnny and Vivian, had taken him to Vegas. John-John, as Cash was known at the time, had begged to play the slots. Vivian had patiently explained that only grown-ups could gamble. But John-John had a few quarters tucked away in a pocket. And when his mother turned around, he stuck one in a machine and pulled the handle. He'd won ten thousand dollars—and Vivian had thought fast and pretended that the quarter had been hers.

Later, when she and his father got him alone, they chided John-John for what he'd done.

His father had announced, "But you know we'll put that money away for you, son. When we get home, we'll open you your own savings account."

This statement was considered humorous in itself, since Johnny Bravo had never saved a cent in his life. If he needed money, he made a deal or placed a bet, and somehow he always came out ahead.

Seven-year-old John-John was a chip off the old block. He looked at his father levelly. "Thanks, Dad. But I'd rather just have the cash."

The way Abby had heard it, no one had ever called him "John-John" again.

Cash got to his feet. "Next week all right? Say, Wednesday? We can go over everything then."

"Sounds fine."

He left, and Abby felt really good. Really positive that they would work through all their difficulties, eventually.

Things weren't going nearly so well with Edna. Already, after just a few days in the same house with her mother, Abby found herself longing to slam a few doors and say some rude things.

It was the same old problem. Edna had been born to make a home. She baked biscuits that dissolved on the tongue and put little plastic sleeves on the pages of her recipe books so no unruly grease spatters would dirty them up.

Abby couldn't fry an egg without breaking the yolk. And her idea of hell would be somewhere that they made you separate the whites from the colors when you did the laundry.

They had started to have their little nitpicky fights again. Edna wanted her new house kept up a certain way. But she wasn't supposed to keep house; she was supposed to take it easy. Keeping house was Abby's job.

Abby tried. She really did. But she could think of a thousand more interesting things to do with herself than dusting the tables or separating the wash. Such as the work Cash had hired her to do. Or reading the *Wall Street Journal* and *U.S. News and World Report*, keeping up on events in the world. Inevitably, when she'd start to do some housewifely chore, she'd end up picking up a book or a calculator. She'd sit down for just a minute or two, perhaps to read about poultry futures; she and Cash had been discussing how much he should have tied up in poultry futures.

The next sound she'd hear would be her mother's querulous voice. "Abigail. Abigail! What are you up to now?"

Her morning sickness, which had seemed to fade during Edna's stay in the hospital, got worse. Her stomach constantly seemed on the verge of rebelling.

Once it did rebel, right at the table, while she and her mother were eating and arguing. She'd had to run for the bathroom. Which had caused no end of questions from Edna when she returned.

"What is the matter with you, Abigail? Are you ill? Is it something you've eaten? I don't understand."

"There's nothing wrong with me."

"What were you doing in the bathroom?"

"Mother. I am fine. Let's just drop it now. Eat your dinner. Please."

"This chicken is bloody. That's probably your problem. E. coli. Or ptomaine."

"I'm fine, Mom. Just fine."

"It's food poisoning. I know it. We should call the clinic right away."

Finally, with continued soothing and groveling, she got Edna settled down. But then, two days later, it happened again; she and Edna argued at the dinner table, and Abby had to run for the bathroom. After that, Abby realized she had to come to grips with her hatred of housework.

She made an effort; she really did. And things started to smooth out a little. Edna found less to complain about. And Abby was scrupulous about not letting arguments get started.

Cash visited on both Saturday and Monday, after that Thursday when he and Abby had met in her office. But those were strictly social calls, for Edna's sake. He chatted with Abby's mother awhile and then left. It seemed to Abby that he avoided talking to her, which she didn't really mind, as she still hadn't worked up the nerve to say what she had to say to him.

She knew she had to stop putting it off. She was in her eleventh week of pregnancy, not showing yet because her stomach was too queasy most of the time for her to put on any weight. She knew very well that she should have seen a doctor a month ago, in Denver. But she'd been walking around in a daze there, working two exhausting jobs, just trying to get through each day as it came along.

She wasn't walking around in a daze anymore. But here at home, she knew everyone at the local clinic. She felt certain they would try to keep the news confidential, but she couldn't see herself showing up there for prenatal care without the word leaking out. And she couldn't bear that: to have Cash or her mother find out the truth from someone else.

They deserved to hear it from her. Cash first. And then Edna.

So, at last, Abby came to a decision. Wednesday, when Cash came to go over the books with her, she would tell him that she carried his child.

He arrived right after lunch and closeted himself with Edna for half an hour. Abby sat up in her office, trying not to bite her fingernails, wishing he would hurry up so they could get down to it.

Then, when she heard his boots on the stairs, she reminded herself of how she was going to handle this: to be cordial and professional while they discussed business, and to keep calm and levelheaded when it came time to break the news.

"Hi." He was standing in the doorway, looking as if he wasn't sure she would let him in.

"Hi." She smiled. He smiled back, cautiously. "Come on in." She had the hard copy of his expense ledger in front of her. "I've got everything ready."

She'd pulled the visitor's chair around to her side of the desk so they could look at the figures together. He frowned at the chair, as if it somehow displeased him. But then he came and dropped into it.

For a few minutes, everything seemed to be going along just fine. They went over the entries, Abby pointing out the places where his natural extravagance should be curbed, asking him why he'd bought certain things at all—making notes as she went so she could move some of the entries to other columns later.

She did find herself terribly distracted by his nearness, by the warmth his body generated, by the smell of his aftershave, which was very faint but nonetheless hard to ignore. Maybe it hadn't been such a good idea to sit next to him. But things had gone so well the week before that she'd become a little complacent about being around him.

She was just nervous enough that she pressed too hard with her pencil when she pointed to a line in the "Travel and Entertainment" column. "What's this?" The lead snapped.

The noise seemed magnified, like a pistol shot in the room. They looked up from the spreadsheet and into each other's eyes.

And it was that night in April all over again. Her whole body leaned toward him.

She knew she had to stop it. She rose from her chair. He stood, too.

She couldn't talk, couldn't say a word. She looked up at him, and he looked down at her. She saw in his eyes what she felt in her heart—and all through her body. A hunger. A yearning.

Memories flooded her. Memories of the two of them. Doing forbidden things.

The humid sweetness of hay was all around her. Zach's favorite mare, Ladybird, snorted nervously in a nearby stall. The wind outside whistled a little as it found its way through the cracks in the walls. And Cash wasn't standing there in front of her, staring into her eyes, but looming above her, his powerful shoulders cutting out the light from the fluorescent lamps overhead, casting the world into seductive shadow.

She had cried out when he covered her, shocked at the heavy, hard feel of him, bewildered at the way he hurt her at first. But the hurt had quickly melted, becoming something altogether different, something wondrous, something frightening, something that lifted her up and turned her inside out. Something that made them more to each other than they had been before—yet less at the same time....

Downstairs, a door slammed, yanking Abby rudely back to the present.

Neither of them moved. They stared at each other, waiting, not breathing.

No other sound came from below.

Cash seemed to shake himself. "I...gotta go." He reached around her, scooped up the papers from her desk. "I'll look these over." He backed away. "And we'll get together again. In a day or two."

She remembered her promise to herself, took a step toward him. "Cash, I want to talk to you. There's something I—"

"No." He held up the hand with the papers in it, warding her off. "Not now. Can't talk now."

"But, Cash, I—"

"Look. I mean it. Gotta go."

"Cash, please. Just listen. Just let me—"

He backed another step, reached behind him for the door. If she hadn't been so desperate, so in conflict within herself, she might have laughed. Cash Bravo was scared to turn his back on her!

"Cash. I'm not kidding. It's important—it really is."

"Not now. I can't talk now. I can't stay here. I have to get out." He yanked open the door, spun on his heel and disappeared.

She just stood there, listening to the heavy tread of his boots as they retreated down the stairs. She heard the front door open and close and then, within moments, his car starting up and driving off. She despised herself a little for not chasing after him. Because she knew he wouldn't visit again for a while—and that until he did, she would put off the grim job of telling him he was going to be a dad.

At his own house, Cash threw some clothes in a bag and left. He drove down to Cheyenne to meet with a few buddies of his. They went to good restaurants and they did a little business.

He returned to Medicine Creek on Monday morning, July 3. He wanted to go over and check on Edna, see if maybe she felt well enough to head over to Ucross for a while tomorrow evening. A tiny town about eighteen miles north of Buffalo, Ucross always put on a nice Independence Day celebration, complete with music and fireworks after dark. He was thinking he'd ask Abby to come, too. There shouldn't be any trouble between them out in the open with Edna along.

Trouble between them. That was how he thought of this…problem he had when it came to Abby. Trouble. Because he couldn't stop thinking about her, in ways that he had no right to think about her. It made no sense. It wasn't like him. He adored women. But he never let himself get crazy over one. Until now. Now he was stark raving out of his head. Over Abby. Of all the women he might have chosen to drive himself nuts over, it had to be her.

He just hoped that, over time, he'd get past it. Hell, he *had* to get past it. She was just an innocent kid and she had her whole life in front of her. And he was a dyed-in-the-wool bachelor, set in his ways. He wanted them to get back to the way they used to be with each other. And they would. Somehow.

He was just reaching for the phone to call Edna, when it rang. He snatched it up and barked into the mouthpiece. "Yeah?"

"Cash? Is that you, Cash?"

The voice was familiar. "Yeah, this is Cash."

"Cash, this is Tess. Tess DeMarley?"

Josh's wife. He smiled into the phone. "Tess. How's everything?"

"Cash, I..."

She hesitated, and all at once he knew she had bad news.

"Tess, what's happened? Is it Jobeth?" Jobeth was her six-year-old daughter.

"No, not Jobeth. She's fine." Tess spoke very carefully. A woman picking her way over a verbal minefield. "It's Josh."

Cash realized he was holding his breath, and let it out in a rush. "What about Josh?"

"He fell from the rig. This morning." She paused, as if composing herself. Then she said it: "Josh is dead."

For a moment, Cash's mind rejected the information. He thought of Ty out under the stars, lifting his thermos of fortified coffee. And Edna, still with them, thank God—but it had been pretty damn scary there for a while. And now Josh? It wasn't possible.

"Cash, I thought you'd want to know." She sounded so calm. But Tess was like that. So young, but still a hell of a woman, one who always kept her head.

He ordered his mind to function. "You sit tight. I'll be there in a few hours."

"Oh, no. You shouldn't..."

He could hear her relief, even as she tried to protest.

"That same apartment? There in Laramie?"

"Cash, it's not your—"

"A few hours. Count on me."

* * *

"Where is Cash lately?" Edna asked. They were at the dinner table.

Abby tried to make her shrug offhand. "I don't know. He's probably away on business."

"It's been days since we heard from him."

"Mom, he has a life."

Edna frowned. "Did something happen between the two of you last Wednesday?"

"Why do you ask that?"

"Well, he left without saying goodbye. And I heard his boots on the stairs. He *ran* down the stairs."

Abby sipped a little tea.

Edna wouldn't be put off. "Well, *did* something happen?"

Abby set down her cup. "No," she lied without remorse. "Not a thing. We went over his expenses. And then he left. He took his ledger sheets with him."

Edna stared at Abby's barely touched plate. "What's happened to your appetite?"

"Mom—"

"No, I've noticed that you've hardly been eating at all since you came back from Denver. And I know that sometimes you don't hold your food down."

"Mom."

"Are you developing an eating disorder of some kind?"

"If you don't stop, I'm getting up and leaving this table."

Edna shook her head. "I don't understand. Cash disappears. And you're not...right. Something's going on. I just want to—"

Abby picked up her plate and started to rise.

"Sit down," Edna said.

After a beat, Abby dropped back into her chair. They ate in silence for a moment.

Then Edna said plaintively, "I just wish you felt you could trust me, whatever it is."

Abby put on a smile. "I do trust you, Mom."

Edna shook her head and turned her attention back to her plate.

Tess wouldn't let Cash pay for the funeral, though he knew she hardly had a dime to her name. And she had no family left, either—none that could help her, anyway. Tess's dad was dead. Her mom lived on Social Security and barely had the funds to make it to Laramie for Josh's funeral. Tess was young, not yet twenty-five, if Cash remembered right. Too young to be widowed and flat broke.

"I'll manage," Tess assured him, smiling that brave smile he'd always admired.

He stayed in Laramie till Saturday morning, through the funeral and the day after, at a hotel not too far from the tiny apartment Tess and her daughter now shared alone. He thought a lot about Josh, about the old days, the good times they used to have. But even more, he worried about Tess and Jobeth. Before he left, he pressed a few bills into Tess's hand, a small enough amount that she could call it a loan and accept it.

She explained, "I've been picking up a few hours here and there down at the corner market. But they told me last week that they'd have to let me go." Her voice turned hopeful. "If you hear of a job in Medicine Creek, something for a woman who might not have a lot of skills but is willing to put in a good day's work...."

He nodded. "I'll see what I can do."

Her eyes hardened. "A job, Cash. Not charity."

And he had to reassure her that there'd be no charity involved.

He was back at his house in Medicine Creek by a little after one in the afternoon. He had a raft of messages on his machine. More than one of them was from Edna.

He dialed her number. She answered on the second ring.

"Hello, Heller residence."

He felt both relief and disappointment that it wasn't Abby who'd answered. "Hi there. How are you doing?"

"Oh, Cash…"

He didn't like the way she sounded. "Edna, are you okay?"

"Of course. I just…I've missed you."

"I'll come right over."

"Yes. Good."

He could have sworn she was crying. "What's the matter?"

She sniffled a little. "Nothing. Everything. Please. I would so like to see you."

He was there in five minutes. And when she opened the door, her red-rimmed eyes said it all. She led him into the living room.

He tried not to ask, but he couldn't help himself. "Where's Abby?"

"Grocery shopping. She'll be back soon." A box of tissues waited on a nearby table. Edna yanked one out and dabbed at her eyes. "So we don't have much time."

"Time for what?"

"To talk."

"Damn it, Edna. What the hell is going on?"

"Oh, I shouldn't say anything. I know it. But I have to talk to someone. And when you called, I was just going crazy, wondering what in the world I was going to do."

"About what?"

Edna dabbed her eyes some more. "I just don't know who else to turn to."

"About what, Edna?"

"It's Abby...."

His mind conjured a million disasters. If someone had hurt her, he'd do murder, he would. He tried to stay cool. "What? What about Abby?"

"She's... Oh, Cash. She will be so angry at me if she learns that I've turned to you about this. But I do count on you. And she won't talk to me."

"Tell me."

Edna smoothed out her tissue, then wadded it up again. "Well, she hasn't been eating much since she came back from Denver. Have you noticed that?"

What did Abby's lack of appetite have to do with disaster? "Yeah. All right. I've noticed."

"And sometimes she gets sick. She goes in the bathroom and she—"

"Fine. I get the point. What are you telling me?"

"I've been over and over it. At first, I thought she was trying to hide an illness. Or maybe an eating disorder. But the past day or two, I've finally admitted to myself what it has to be."

"What?"

"Oh, I'm so worried for her. But why else would she take off for Denver like that, with hardly a word of explanation? And why, once she got there, would she refuse to return our calls? Refuse to come home until her own mother was at death's door? Even now, she won't confide in me. Won't turn to me. She always thinks she has to handle everything herself, has to shoulder all the burden alone. Ever since she was a tiny thing, it was that way. She wouldn't—"

"Edna. What the hell is wrong with Abby?"

Edna gulped. "Oh, Cash."

"What? God. Tell me."

Edna closed her eyes. A shudder racked her slim shoulders. And then she hung her head. "She's pregnant. Isn't it obvious? She's pregnant. Some awful man has taken advantage of her and then left her to deal with the consequences all on her own."

Chapter Five

Abby saw Cash's Cadillac in front of the house when she turned onto Meadowlark Lane.

So, she thought grimly, wherever he's been, he's back.

This time, she decided, she would tell him the truth before he could get away—if she had to shout it at his back as he tried to run out the door. She pulled into the driveway and opened the garage door with the remote control. Then she slid the Rabbit in beside her mother's old station wagon.

Carrying a bag of groceries in each arm, she entered through the kitchen.

"Abigail!" her mother called from the living room.

Abby slid the groceries onto the end of the counter. "Coming!" She smoothed her hands down her jeans, pulled her shoulders back and marched into the other room.

Cash stood from an easy chair as she entered. Their eyes met.

And she knew that he knew.

Two steps and he was beside her, taking her arm. "Let's go."

She stared at him, her mind gone suddenly to mush. "Go where?"

"My house. We have to talk. Alone."

Edna, in the other easy chair, started sputtering. "Cash, no. Really, I didn't mean for you to—"

"Edna, don't worry. I'll handle this." He started pulling Abby toward the front door. "Come on."

Abby dug in her heels. "What is going on?" she demanded, as if she didn't already know.

Edna stood, putting her hand to her heart. "Oh, Abigail. I was so worried about you. I *had* to talk to someone...."

Cash turned to Edna then, his concern for her health crowding out his determination to get Abby alone. "Now, settle down, Edna. I'm going to fix everything—you'll see. I just want you to trust me. I don't want you to get yourself too worked up about this."

Abby clenched her teeth so hard she wondered why they didn't crack. "Worked up about what?"

"Oh, Abigail," Edna cried in abject misery, "why is it you've never felt you could talk to me?"

Abby sucked in a deep breath and let it out slowly. Then she spoke with great patience. "Mother, go lie down."

"No, no. We have to *talk* about this."

"We will. When I get back."

"Back from where?"

"Cash's house."

"But that's not right. Cash has nothing to do with this."

"He really wants to be involved." She sent Cash a telling glance. "Don't you, Cash?"

His eyes bored through her. "That's right. I really do."

"Oh." Edna wrung her hands. "I feel so useless. I had to talk to someone. And then Cash called. And I—"

"Shh," Abby soothed. "You are not to worry. I promise. It will all work out."

"Oh, honey…"

Taking her mother by the hand, Abby headed for the downstairs bedroom. Once she got there, she led Edna straight to the bed. "Come on. Sit."

Obedient as a child, Edna dropped to the edge of the bed. Abby knelt, slipped off her mother's house shoes and helped her to stretch out. Then Abby stood. "We'll be at Cash's. And you will be fine. If you just rest."

"Abigail."

"What?"

"Are you going to have a baby?"

The time for denials had passed. "Yes, Mom."

A whimper escaped Edna. "Oh, dear…"

"Rest. Please. It will be okay."

"I should be more help."

"Just rest. That will help a lot—I promise you."

Edna sighed, a deep, weary sigh. "You'll be at Cash's?"

"Yes."

"Cash will help you. Cash always helps."

"Yes. He does. And he will. You'll see."

"All right, then." Edna closed her eyes. "We'll talk when you get back from Cash's."

Abby turned. Cash was standing in the doorway to the hall.

"Let's go," he said.

* * *

"Why the hell didn't you tell me?" he demanded, as soon as they were alone in his big living room, with its plush area rugs, soaring windows and vaulted ceiling.

"Cash, listen—"

He paced the floor. "You lied to me. I asked you directly in Denver. I said, 'Are you pregnant?' and you looked me straight in the eye and you told me no."

"I wasn't ready to talk about it then."

Cash stopped pacing and raked a hand back through his hair. "Hell. How could I not have figured it out? The way you eat. That tea you're always drinking. And the way you look so skinny and green." She was standing in front of the long, off-white sofa, opposite him. He frowned at her across the coffee table. "Are you all right?"

Abby sighed and dropped to the sofa. "I'm fine. And my mother should have come to me first."

Cash made a snorting sound. "You know she could never talk to you." He marched to a caramel-colored leather chair a few feet away and sat down. "She doesn't know I'm the father." He braced his elbows on his knees and hung his head in shame. "God help me, I didn't have the guts to tell her. It's going to break her heart. I've abused the trust she and Ty had in me." He studied his boots for a moment, then he glanced up and into her eyes. "Let alone the trust *you* had in me."

She held his gaze firmly. "It *is* your baby, Cash."

Now he looked injured. "How could you think I would doubt it?"

"I just wanted to say it. I've been meaning to say it. Trying to say it."

"Abby..." He didn't seem to know how to go on.

"It *is* your baby," she said again. "And I want it. I do."

His eyes darkened. "What does that mean? Did you think I would try to stop you from having it?"

"No, I never thought that." She leaned forward, to the edge of the sofa, willing him to understand, to see how it had been for her. "It's just that I've been trying to figure out a way to tell you for what seems like forever now."

"Well." He looked grim. "Now I know."

She felt defiant. "And I'm *glad* you know—even if my mother was the one who ended up telling you."

He stared at her for a long moment, then he turned and flipped open a little carved box that sat on a small table by his chair. He took out a cigarette and tapped it on the edge of the table. Then, the cigarette poised in mid-tap, he shot her a reproving glance. "You should have come to me." With a low oath, he tossed the cigarette back in the box. "But then, how the hell could you?" He snapped the lid of the box shut. "How could you turn to me ever again after I—"

She stood then. "Cash Bravo."

He scowled at her. "What?"

"You've got to stop beating yourself up about this. You have to remember how it was that night. I was...willing. More than willing. No matter how much you want all the blame, you can't have it."

He was shaking his head. "You're only a—"

She glared at him. "If you call me a kid, I will do serious bodily harm to you."

He glared back, but only for a moment. Then he was looking at his boots again. "I know you hate me."

"When will you hear me? I do not hate you."

"I'm too old for you, I know."

At first, she didn't realize what he was getting at. "What does how old you are have to do with anything?"

"Abby...." He looked so sad, a man on a first-name basis with regret. He got to his feet and walked over to the tall windows at the end of the room. Outside, the wind filled the air with feathery white fluff from the cottonwood trees. The sun shone down. In the distance, however, toward the Big Horns, dark-bellied clouds loomed. Cash looked out for a moment, at the distant clouds and the whirling white fluff. And then he turned. "I think it's best if we get married."

She swallowed. It was exactly what she'd expected he would say. Still, it had the power to surprise her. "What?"

"You heard me. We'll get married."

She drew herself up, tried to sound firm. "No. No, really. We can't do that."

"The hell we can't."

"Listen. I mean it. It would be a mistake—you know it would."

He shrugged, as if her words had meant nothing. "It's the right thing. And we'll do it."

She came out from behind the coffee table, into the middle of the room. "Cash, you're not listening to me."

"Yes, I am."

"Then hear what I'm telling you. I won't marry you. It never works when people get married for something like this."

He looked at her as if she'd said something incredibly foolish and juvenile. Then he replied quietly, "You'll marry me."

She shook her head. "No. It's not a good idea."

A weary half smile tugged on one corner of his mouth. "Why not?"

"I just...well, I don't think it's wise."

That half smile remained, making him look infinitely superior and worldly-wise. "You're twenty-one. You don't know a thing about wisdom." He strode to her and took her by the shoulders.

His touch felt so good. And she was so...confused. This wasn't working out. Instead of marshaling her very reasonable arguments against marrying him and laying them before him with calm self-assurance, she'd stammered and hesitated. She hadn't been convincing at all.

And he had just plain refused to listen to her.

She glanced away from him, toward the window. Out there, the air was heavy and moist—charged with the promise of a summer storm.

"Look at me."

She did, putting considerable effort into keeping her expression severe and composed.

"We'll get married," Cash said. "We'll make the best of it. It's better for the baby. Can't you see that?"

Abby shrugged free of his grip and moved around him, toward the window.

He spoke to her back. "The baby deserves whatever we can give him. And we can give him two parents who did their best to make a marriage between them, to make a family for him."

She looked out at the blowing cottonwood fluff and the slowly darkening sky.

"Abby, come on. You know it's the best thing—the *right* thing—to do."

She watched lightning fork down, and heard the thunder boom out far away somewhere.

"Abby..."

She spoke, but it was more to herself than to him. "I

never wanted to be a wife. I wanted…to work with you. And to run my own life."

He came up behind her, but he didn't touch her. She could feel him standing there. "I know, Abby. And I do understand."

She smiled to herself. "I'll bet."

"What's that supposed to mean?"

Lightning flashed again. The dark clouds boiled in. "I just know you. I know how you are."

"How?"

She could hear the wind keening.

"How am I, Abby?"

She turned to him. "You're a bachelor to the core. You've never in your life wanted to get married, to anyone." She paused, halfway hoping that he would argue. But he didn't argue. So she went on, "Oh, you love the way all the women go gaga over you. And you treat them all so nice. But marriage has never been of much interest to you. You like your wheeling and your dealing. You like to get up and go when the mood strikes. You want to be free to follow a deal—or to ride out in your Cadillac to rescue some needy friend. You're everyone's knight in shining armor. But you're just not the marrying kind."

She could see by his expression that she had described him personally. And it made her sad, somehow. So very sad.

"Fine," he said. "We both like being single—but now you're going to have a baby. A baby you say you want."

She pushed the sadness away and replied with assurance, "I don't just *say* it. I *do* want it."

"Then think of the baby. Do what's right. Marry me."

"It will never work." Even as she said it, she was waiting for him to come back strong, to argue that it *would* work. That they would *make* it work.

He cleared his throat. "It might."

She cast a put-upon glance toward the vaulted ceiling. "You sound *so* convincing."

He grunted. "Well, all right. Maybe it won't work. In the long run. And if it doesn't work…"

"What?"

"Abby, people do get divorced."

For some reason, that hurt. To have him already planning divorce when she hadn't even agreed to marry him. She stared up at him—and found herself thinking about how much she liked looking at him.

It made her feel good to look at him. As if all was right with the world. But she supposed that made sense. He'd always been there, in her world. The family story went that he'd held her in his arms shortly after she was born. All her life, she had counted on him. And confided in him. She had always known that she could tell him anything.

And it had been so hard these past grim weeks, feeling as if she didn't dare talk to him at all. But now, the long silence had been broken. They were saying things that had to be said. True, it didn't approach the old easiness they used to share. But it was something, at least.

And she had known that he'd demand marriage. What she hadn't expected was to hear him speak so calmly of divorce

She edged around him again, moving out into the middle of the room, where she turned and faced him squarely. "So you're not talking about a *real* marriage at all. Just a marriage on paper. You want to set it up so that when our baby asks about it later, it will look like we cared."

He frowned. "That is not what I said. I said we'd try."

"'Try.'" She braced her hands on her hips. "That's a puny little word if I ever heard one."

"Abby, you're fifteen years younger than I am. And you just said yourself that you never wanted to be a wife." He held out both arms to the sides. "And look here. See any strings? No, you don't. Because I like being single. It's just what you said. We're neither of us the marrying kind." He approached her again, cautiously. "Together we probably haven't got a snowflake's chance in hell of making a marriage last."

"Well, it's good to see you have such confidence in us." She started to turn.

He caught her arm. "Don't get cute."

She shook him off, but stood her ground. "I am not cute."

"Look, I know I did wrong by you."

"There you go again. Acting like I wasn't even there."

"But I want to do right by my child—as well as by the woman who is carrying my child."

"Cash, did you hear yourself? You just called me a *woman*. Are we making progress here?"

His eyes glinted dangerously. "You will marry me, Abby." He took her by the shoulders again. "Say you will." He pulled her marginally closer. She felt his strength, his determination to do what he thought was right. His breath across her face was warm, and a little uneven. "Say yes."

She knew at that moment that she *would* say yes. She even had enough self-awareness to realize that she *wanted* to say yes.

But some contrary devil inside her couldn't just give in and go along. She had to push it a little, to find out exactly how much he counted on the option of divorce.

"Did you mean that? About getting divorced if it doesn't work out?"

His eyes were like mirrors, giving only her own reflection back to her. "Yeah, I meant it."

"Then maybe we should just admit what we're doing. From the first."

He blinked. "You've lost me."

"I mean, we could have an agreement between the two of us, right up front. The marriage would last until the baby comes. Or a little after. A year, say. We could be married for a year. And then, unless we change our minds and both decide we *are* the marrying kind, I'll go to Reno twelve months after our wedding day—and get a divorce. And after that, we will equally share custody of our child."

He stared at her, his eyes wary. "Is that what you want?"

It wasn't, not really. In spite of the way she'd scoffed when he'd said it, she would have preferred to leave things open-ended: to simply give the marriage an honest try. But what right did she have to tie Cash down permanently if he didn't want to be tied down? Wouldn't he be happier if he knew he could easily be free within a year? When she looked at it that way, her proposal didn't seem like such a bad idea. The local scandal would be minimized, because the marriage would serve as a public statement that both the mother and the father were committed to the child they'd made. And if it didn't last, well, people in Medicine Creek accepted divorce these days more readily than they accepted unwed mothers and illegitimate kids.

"It could work," Abby said.

"I asked you if it's what you want." His eyes challenged her.

Abby Heller had never been one to turn down a challenge. "Yes. It's what I want." Her voice sounded so sure, much more sure than she felt.

Idly, he brushed his thumbs along the sides of her neck. "It would have to be just between us, this agreement."

Down inside her something heated and pooled. She tried to ignore it, tried to keep her voice matter-of-fact. "That's what I said."

He went on stroking the sides of her neck—so lightly. "Fine. What 'between us' means to me is that no one else would know about it."

"Agreed." She tried to pull away.

He held on—so gently. "I'm not finished."

"Okay. What else?"

He caressed the tip of her chin. Resolute, she neither flinched nor sighed.

"We would also live together for the year. And for that time, it would be a real marriage." He put both hands solidly on her shoulders again, his expression grave. "We'd give it an honest try."

Something happened inside her, a little burst of joy. Because he did want to try. He wanted a real marriage, for as long as it lasted. She did her best to look sure of herself—and to stop thinking about his idle caresses, caresses that he probably didn't even realize aroused her. "Yes, all right. An honest try. But in a year, unless we both change our minds, it's over."

He frowned, dropped his hands from her shoulders and stepped back. "Would you want it in writing?"

She smiled, a businesslike smile. "I'll take your word—if you'll take mine."

He nodded. "Good enough." He held out his hand.

They shook to seal the bargain as outside lightning

flashed, thunder boomed and the first drops of rain began to fall.

They made sure Edna was resting comfortably when they told her that Cash was the father of Abby's baby and that they were getting married right away.

But Edna surprised them both. After a few agonizing seconds where she stared in openmouthed disbelief from her daughter to Cash and then back to her daughter again, she smiled.

A slow smile. "Well." She went on smiling. "This isn't so bad after all—now, is it?"

Abby didn't like that smile at all. "What do you mean, it's not so bad?"

"Well, now, Abigail, we all know how you are."

"Oh. And how is that?"

"Headstrong, to put it mildly. Headstrong and rash."

"So?"

"So at least you were headstrong and rash with the right man."

Abby couldn't come up with a scathing enough reply for that one.

Edna went one better. "And you need a man strong enough to master you."

Abby groaned. "*Master* me?" She thought she heard Cash chuckle, but when she shot him a glance, his face was perfectly serious. She turned her attention to Edna again. "I do not believe you said that."

Edna huffed a little. "You did ask."

"And I regret asking, believe me."

"Also, Cash will take care of you."

"I can take care of myself."

Edna wasn't listening. "And we'll all be a family," she said. "At last. In the real, true sense. Cash's children will be my grandchildren. Nate and Zach will be their uncles.''

She held out her hand—toward Cash, Abby realized. He stepped forward, still looking appropriately grave, and took that outstretched hand.

"Oh, Cash, I'm so happy. This is wonderful. I'm just...overwhelmed with joy.''

Chapter Six

Two weeks later, on July 22, Cash and Abby were married in the neat little white-trimmed brick church where each of them had been baptized as children. Abby wore the dress in which Vivian Sellerby had wed Johnny Bravo thirty-eight years before, a stunning creation of silk and seed pearls, with a basque waist and lace sleeves that came to pearl-embroidered points on the tops of her hands. The dress was a pretty good fit, except for the waist, which had to be let out at the last minute to allow for the weight that Abby had finally started to put on.

The church was full. Of course the whole town had been talking; no one had ever thought there was *that* kind of relationship between Cash and Abby. In the days after the word got out, Abby had been congratulated frequently on her upcoming marriage. To her, some of those congratulations seemed a little forced, especially from the other single women in town. Though Cash had never come close to proposing to any of them, more than one had dared to dream that someday she would be his chosen bride.

They held the reception at Cash's house. Cash had hired a caterer from Sheridan, a small woman with a big ability to put a great party together in a hurry. She had the rugs rolled back in the living room and had hired a four-piece band. She'd put tubs of bright flowers everywhere, decorated the banisters with white silk roses that looked like the real thing and prepared a feast that included Rising Sun beef, lobster on ice and game birds stuffed with corn bread and chestnuts. The cake had four tiers and raspberry sauce between the layers.

Abby danced the first dance with Cash's father. Johnny Bravo had arrived the day before from some small South American country where he'd been enjoying retirement for the past few years. He looked like an older version of Cash: tan, fit and heartbreaker-handsome—and not a day over fifty, though his actual age was sixty-six. He'd brought along his new wife, his fourth. Her name was Allegra. Allegra spoke with a faint accent, one Abby couldn't place. She had platinum-blond hair and eyes the tropical green of a parrot's wing. She resembled the pop singer Madonna. A very young Madonna. If Allegra was over twenty-five, Abby would eat her wedding veil.

"You look beautiful," Johnny told Abby as she whirled in his arms. He seemed a little misty-eyed, and a little sad, too. Abby wondered if it bothered him that she had chosen to wear Vivian's wedding gown.

Everyone said that Vivian had been the great love of Johnny Bravo's life. She had died giving birth to their second child, a girl. The baby hadn't made it, either. People said Johnny had never gotten over the loss, and that his relationships with all the other women who came after were only pitiful attempts to get through the rest of his life without the woman he loved.

Abby wanted him to understand why she'd chosen the dress. "I always admired this dress, from the pictures of you and Vivian. And Mom remembered that it was up in the attic at the ranch. I guess it just seemed like a good idea to wear it today."

Johnny gave her a big smile. "There's no need to explain. Viv would have been honored that you chose that dress. And I am honored, too."

"Well, I'm glad, then."

When the dance ended, Cash came to claim her. Before he did, Johnny whispered in her ear, "My son's a lucky devil. You be happy, you hear?"

She whispered back, "I will."

Another tune started up. Cash took her in his arms. For a moment, they simply danced. Smiling, Abby closed her eyes and leaned her head on her husband's shoulder. She felt all shimmery. For the past two weeks, she'd been getting used to the idea that Cash would be her husband. It really hadn't been that difficult an adjustment after all.

"You seem happy," he said.

His voice was soft and teasing in her ear. She liked the sound of it. She also liked the feel of his arms, guiding her in the dance.

She cuddled a little closer to him. "It was a nice wedding. And this is a nice party."

"But are you happy? Right now, at this minute?"

"Yes. I am."

"Well, good. I want you to be happy."

They danced some more. Abby went on thinking about how right it felt, to dance with Cash. But that shouldn't have surprised her. He had taught her to dance, after all, in the great room of the ranch house. He could dance to anything. From Glenn Miller to Billy Ray Cyrus, the fox trot to the achy-breaky. The first time he showed her how to waltz, she had stood on his feet as he glided her around the floor; she had felt as if she were floating on air.

"What?" he asked.

"What do you mean, what?"

"That dreamy look, that's what."

"Just thinking. Remembering."

"Remembering what?"

"Me standing on your feet, learning to dance."

He chuckled. "You learned fast."

"I'm a bright girl."

He pulled her close again and they finished out the dance. After that, he spoke to the boys in the band. They played a slow, stately number. Cash went to Edna and held out his hand. She rose and allowed her new son-in-law to squire her out onto the floor.

Abby danced with Zach and then with Nate, who had come all the way from Los Angeles for this event. As usual, Nate's black hair grew over his collar. Abby smoothed it a little, thinking how handsome and dangerous and semidisreputable he looked. Nate had always had a reputation as a bad boy. But Abby had grown up with him. She knew he wasn't nearly as bad as he liked everyone to think.

"If I'd known Cash would snap you up, I would have made a play myself," Nate said teasingly.

"Well, it's too late now."

"You let me know if he gives you any grief."

She faked a look of surprise. "Cash? Give me grief?"

He grunted. "He's a lucky son of a gun."

"His father said that, too. Apparently, I'm a real prize.

I hate housekeeping and I can't cook. But there's something wonderful about me anyway.''

Nate lifted an eyebrow at her and she realized from his expression that he'd guessed there was a child on the way. Well, what could she expect? After all, she *was* beginning to show. And she imagined a lot of people must have noticed—and remarked on it when they thought she wouldn't hear. And surely by the time she bore a full-term baby just six months after her wedding day anyone who could count would have figured it out.

She grinned defiantly up at Nate.

Nate tossed back his head and laughed out loud. But when he looked down at her again, his dark eyes had grown serious. "You mean the world to him. And I know that scares him. Don't let it scare you off."

Before Abby could think of what to say to that, they danced past Meggie May Kane, whose father owned a smaller ranch bordering Rising Sun land. Abby saw the swift, hot look that passed between Nate and Meggie.

Years ago, Nate and Meggie had been friends. But not anymore. Now they went out of their way to avoid each other whenever Nate came to town. Abby thought it was too bad. She had seen with her own eyes how strongly they were drawn to each other. That had been years ago, when they were both nineteen and Abby was just a little girl, crouching in the bushes, spying on her elders.

The dance ended. Barnaby Cotes, a local shop owner, was waiting for a dance with the bride. As he stepped in, Nate turned and walked away.

A little while later, the band took a break. Abby wandered over to the bar, where Tess DeMarley assisted the bartender by serving the punch and soft drinks.

Tess had come to town just last week, after Cash had called her and explained that Abby's mother needed a housemate. Tess would get food and board and a small salary for looking after Edna, taking care of the house and cooking the meals. And there was a gift shop in town that would hire her if she wanted more work as Edna's health improved.

Abby had never thought Edna would go for it. She couldn't see her mother letting any stranger—especially one with a child—move into her beloved house. But Tess DeMarley was gentle and soft-spoken, a great cook and a fine housekeeper. Edna had taken one look at her and known she'd found the daughter that Abby should have been. So Edna was as happy as a bee in clover. She even got along with Tess's quiet, self-possessed daughter, Jobeth.

Abby liked Tess, too. Who could help but like her? She had a sort of ingrained dignity and goodness about her. Yet she wasn't self-righteous in the least. She'd had a tough life, living with that reckless Josh DeMarley all those years. And now she was a widow, starting all over again.

"Punch?" Tess asked.

"I'd love some."

Tess dipped up some punch and handed Abby a cup.

Abby took a long, grateful drink. "I haven't seen you dance once."

Tess looked down modestly. "I've been busy helping out."

Just then, Zach wandered by. Abby reached out and grabbed him. "I want you to dance with Tess. Now."

Tess looked all flustered. "Oh, no. Really...."

"I'd be pleased to," Zach said, and held out his hand.

"Go on," Abby instructed. "It's my wedding. And I'll mind the punch bowl. Don't you worry about a thing." She watched, smiling fatuously, as tall, quiet Zach danced off with pretty, reserved Tess. She thought they made a nice couple. Who could say? Maybe she and Cash would start a trend, a rash of Bravo weddings. Zach would marry Tess. And Nate would finally get together with Meggie May Kane.

She told Cash about her matchmaking fantasies later, after midnight, when the guests had all gone and the little dynamo of a caterer had packed everything up and driven away. Cash grinned when she told him. But then he shook his head. "Nate's favorite song is 'Don't Fence Me In.' And you know Meggie May—she'll never leave the Double-K. It's got fences all around it. And as for Zach..." He let silence finish the sentence.

Abby took his meaning. Zach had married his high-school sweetheart, Leila Wickerston, a week after graduation. The marriage lasted three years. When Leila walked out, she took their only child with her. "It's been years since Leila left him. He *might* try again."

Cash only grunted. He went over to the bar, clear now of all the party paraphernalia, and poured himself two fingers of Jack Daniels. He sipped, leaning against the bar, regarding her over the rim of his glass.

She regarded him right back.

A long, slow moment went by before he seemed to shake himself. "It's late," he said. "I'll bet you're tired."

She shook her head. "No, I'm not tired. Not at all." She felt like the heroine of *My Fair Lady*—she wanted to dance all night.

Or make love.

She smiled to herself. It was true. She wanted to make love with Cash again. She'd had two weeks to deal with the idea. Like the idea of being his wife, it hadn't been that hard to get used to.

She was sitting on the couch, still in her wedding gown, though she'd long ago dispensed with the veil. She stood. "I don't know what's the matter with this dress."

He sipped some more. "There's not a damn thing wrong with that dress."

His voice sounded gruff. Deliciously so.

"For some reason, it seems a little tight."

"You're finally starting to put on some weight."

She approached him slowly. "I'll be as round as a water barrel before you know it."

He stayed where he was, but his big body seemed to tense. "You look good."

Now he sounded grim.

"Well. Thank you."

He saluted her with his glass, then drained the last of his drink.

She took the glass from his hand and set it on the bar. "You'll have to undo me."

He coughed. "Huh?"

She turned around and showed him the back of the dress. "Undo me."

For a moment, he did nothing. And then she felt his fingers on the topmost pearl button. It took several minutes; it was a long row of buttons. But finally, he'd undone each one.

Abby breathed deeply for the first time in hours. "Umm. That feels wonderful."

She turned to find him watching her. Intently. She smiled.

He didn't smile back. "Go on to bed."

She frowned—and then she understood. "Oh. I'm supposed to slip into something more comfortable, is that it? And then you'll join me in a few minutes?"

He said nothing. Not a good sign.

The pleasant, hazy feeling of sensual anticipation began to fade. "Okay. What is it? What's wrong?"

"Nothing."

She stared at him for a moment. Then she muttered, "Major lie."

He reached for the bottle of Jack Daniels again. "Just go to bed."

She watched him pour. "No."

He set the bottle down too hard. "Damn it, Abby." He drank, looked away, then back. "Why don't you just let it go?"

"Let it go? Are you crazy?"

He plunked down his glass. "This is ridiculous."

"No argument."

"Then go to bed."

"No way. I'm your wife. And this is our wedding night."

He gave her a long, hard stare. When that didn't work, he sighed. "Just go to bed."

"No. Forget it. I'm not putting up with this."

"Putting up with *what?*"

She put her hands on her hips—to show him her exasperation, as well as to keep her dress from falling off. "We agreed to a real marriage, Cash. For however long it lasts. It's our wedding night. And on their wedding night, people in a real marriage make love."

"Abby, don't push me."

She closed her eyes and counted to ten. Then she mustered all her courage and dared to demand, "Are you saying you don't want to make love with me?"

"Abby, I—"

"Just answer the question. Do you or don't you?"

"Abby..."

"My name is not an answer."

"I just think…"

"What? You just think what?"

"That it's wrong for me to take advantage of you."

"Cash, get this—*I really want to be taken advantage of.*"

"You say that now."

"And I mean it. You're not going to prove anything by staying away from me." She paused long enough to slant him a sideways look. "Except maybe that you don't really want to give our marriage an honest chance."

His golden brows drew together. "You're twisting what I said. Of course I mean to give this marriage an honest chance. But you're just a—"

She put up a hand. "Do not say it. Please. Look at the facts. I'm legally an adult. Old enough to drink. Old enough to vote. Old enough to have your baby, Cash Bravo. Which is exactly what I'm going to be doing some time in the middle of January."

He shook his head wearily. She had no idea what was happening in his mind.

"What?" she demanded at last. "Say something."

"I want a cigarette."

She turned around, flounced over to the little carved box by the caramel-colored leather chair and got him one. Then she flounced back, clutching her dress against her breasts with her free hand. "Here." She held it out.

He looked at it. "It's bad for me."

She granted him a look of infinite patience as she tossed it on the bar. Her dress slid off one shoulder. She yanked it up. "This thing is driving me nuts." She slanted another glance at Cash. "I'm taking it off."

"Abby…"

She stuck a finger under the neckline and gave a little tug. It dropped off of her shoulders. Unfortunately, the long, pearl-embroidered lace sleeves were too snug to slide easily down her arms. She looked down at herself. "Trapped. In my own wedding gown."

"I can see that."

Abby froze. She looked up into Cash's eyes. She saw equal parts humor and heat.

And she thought again of dancing. That she and Cash were dancing. He had almost walked off the floor. But she had held him there, somehow. And the music between them was beguiling him once more. The important thing right now was that she not stumble, not miss a step.

She wrinkled her nose, keeping the mood playful, keeping it light. "Give me a minute here." She took her sweet time, peeling the sleeves free of her arms. That accomplished, she let the dress fall to the floor. She stepped out of it slowly, then picked it up and carried it to a chair. There, she laid it out with great care. It was a lot more of a fuss than she ordinarily would have made over a dress. But this wasn't just any dress.

And besides, the process of laying it out, of smoothing the delicate silk, had become part of the dance she and Cash were sharing. When she straightened and looked at Cash again, he hadn't moved from where she'd left him.

"Pretty slip," he said.

She looked down at her floor-length ivory satin slip, then back up at him. "Thank you."

"Welcome."

She felt awkward, suddenly. She touched the shimmery fabric of the dress again, for reassurance, and spoke shyly, not looking at him. "Your dad said your mother would have liked it. That I wore her dress."

"Who knows what goes on with him?"

She looked up and saw him shrug, a shrug that dismissed her words—and discouraged further discussion on the topic of his father.

"You never would talk much about your dad," she said. In her heart, she thought he resented the way his dad had left him when Vivian died all those years ago. But they'd never really gone into it. Whenever Abby would bring up the subject of Johnny Bravo, Cash would always say it was useless to dwell on the past.

He said it now. "What's the point? It's history."

"He introduced me to Allegra," Abby said carefully. "She seemed nice. And I really think she's crazy about him."

Cash made a low sound in his throat. "Oh, come on. She could be his *granddaughter.*"

"But she's not. She's his wife."

"For the moment."

"Cash, you're so cynical."

"Realistic is more like it."

"And you're too hung up on age differences."

He actually chuckled. "Have you been taking psychology courses at C.U. when I wasn't looking?"

"No. Strictly business administration." She put up a hand. "I do solemnly swear."

"Good. I don't need you analyzing me."

"But I do analyze you. Lately, anyway."

"What the hell for?"

"Because..." She wasn't sure how to explain.

"Yeah?"

"Oh, because I've always taken you for granted, I guess. Like my father or my mother. Like Zach and Nate. Only more so. You've always been there whenever I needed you. Like air. Or water. Like food. And then, for a while, you weren't there."

"Because you wouldn't let me be."

He sounded angry.

She longed for him to understand. "Because I *couldn't* let you be."

"You could have. You could have always come to me. And you should have."

"No, I couldn't."

"Yes, you could."

"Let's not argue. Please?"

He leaned on the bar and picked up the cigarette she'd dropped there. "Fine with me."

She smiled, a smile she knew quivered a little at the corners. And she bravely announced, "I want my wedding night, Cash."

He tossed the cigarette down again.

"Well? Are you going to give it to me?"

He said nothing. Treading carefully, she closed the distance between them.

When she stood in front of him, she gazed up at him in honest appeal. "Say something. Please?"

He lifted a hand and touched the side of her face. Then, hesitantly, he asked, "You're sure that this is what you want?"

She shivered a little. His slightest touch seemed to burn her, to start off fires down below. "Yes."

He caressed her cheek, a long, slow stroke, over the rounded ridge of her cheekbone and down to the curve of her chin. "You won't go running off this time afterward?"

"No."

"Swear it."

"I swear."

"Whatever happens—now or in the future. You won't run away from me. Ever again."

She shook her head.

"Say it. Say you won't."

"I won't, Cash. I promise you. I won't run away from you ever again."

"All right, then."

She waited, holding her breath.

And then, at last, his hand strayed down, over her neck, out to her shoulder, where he slid his finger under the thin satin strap of her slip. He lifted the strap, lowered it back in place. "I think about that night all the time."

She let out the breath she was holding, but didn't dare to speak.

He lifted the strap again, guided it over the slope of her shoulder and let it fall down her arm. "That day in your office, I had to get out. I wanted to kiss you then. I wanted to do a lot more than kiss you."

She said nothing, only listened. And reveled in sensation. She loved the feel of the silky strap against her arm. And the weight of the slip, uneven now, since the top of one side had fallen down. She didn't look to see, but she could feel that the top swell of her left breast was exposed, as well as the tiny scrap of lace she wore for a bra.

Cash hooked up the other strap, guided it down her other arm. He pulled on that strap. She helped him, sliding her arms up and clear of both straps, then letting them fall to her sides once more. The slip slithered to her waist and stopped there, held up by the swell of her hips below.

"Pretty," he said. He touched her bare skin, at the top of her belly, between her bra and the slip. Her stomach tightened in response. He smiled, a lazy, knowing smile.

She felt as if she were melting, slowly, from the inside out. "Oh, Cash…"

"Shh." He brushed his fingers against her lips.

She obeyed his command, falling silent.

He touched the strap of her bra. "So pretty."

She ordered her suddenly wobbly legs to hold her upright as his finger slid down, tracing the skin along the edge of the bra strap, caressing the slope of her left breast. She shivered and sighed. He was still smiling, his sexiest smile. His eyes were like smoke.

Now *this* was dancing, she thought. Dancing in the truest sense. Right in tune, in perfect rhythm. Though neither of them had taken a step.

His finger moved on, to the center of her chest, and then up the rounded swell of her other breast.

She captured his hand, guided it to her mouth and pressed her lips into his palm.

His hand escaped her grasp, to slide around and cup her nape. He said her name on a breath.

And then he reeled her in.

Chapter Seven

Cash's fingers threaded up into her hair, beneath the tiny silk flowers woven there. He pulled her up into him. She went, lifting on tiptoe.

His mouth settled over hers, stealing her breath and then giving it back to her. She heard a moan—hers or his, she couldn't be sure.

He kissed her long and slow and deep, taking his time, tasting her, savoring her. And she let him do that, wanted him to do that. She hovered on tiptoe, her arms limp at her sides, and held her mouth up to him, sighing in delight as he took what she offered.

They kissed for the longest time, standing there in the middle of the living room. He undressed her as he kissed her, putting his big hands on the sides of her hips, sliding down the satin slip, making of the action one long, slow caress. They both sighed as the satin fell away to land around her ankles.

His lips played on hers, his tongue hungry and seeking, as he unhooked her bra and tossed it away. Her breasts, so heavy and hot, yearned for his touch. He gave her that touch, cupping them, seeming to ease the yearning for a moment, and then only managing to increase it.

His hands roamed over her flesh as his mouth plundered hers. It was heaven. Could this be real? After midnight on her wedding night. Standing here in Cash's living room, wearing nothing but her diamond ring, her panty hose and her satin shoes.

Kissing Cash.

Making love...

He lifted his mouth from hers.

"Let's go to bed." His voice caressed her, rough and tender. He lifted an eyebrow as if to say, Well?

She gulped and nodded, staring up at his mouth, which looked swollen from kissing her.

He scooped her up against his chest and carried her to the master bedroom, which was through a short hall off the living room. She kicked off her shoes as he bore her down the hall and heard them bump the wall when they fell.

In the room, he carried her straight to the bed, gently laid her down and turned a dial on the wall. The two lamps on either side of the bed came on very low. Swiftly, he got rid of his own clothes: the black silk tux, the stiff white shirt, the trousers, the black dress shoes. Everything. All of it.

He lay down with her, on his huge bed with its maple bedstead and its bold, red-and-blue-patterned comforter. He reached for her, wrapping his strong arms around her, then pulling back just enough to help her with her panty hose. By then, they were both too needful to go slowly; the panty hose tore. Neither of them cared.

When she was totally nude, he put his hand on her belly, felt its roundness. And on her breast again. "Fuller," he said.

She nuzzled him, claiming his mouth once more. He kissed her as she wanted to be kissed, slow and open and wet. And as he kissed her, his hand went roving, over her fuller breasts and her rounder belly and down, to the place where her thighs joined. His fingers delved in.

She gasped. He moaned into her mouth. She moved against him, urging him on, transported by the wondrous sensations of his hands and lips upon her burning skin.

He pulled his mouth from hers, looked down into her eyes. She saw bewilderment. And a need as strong and consuming as her own.

"Abby, I'm sorry. Can't wait. Don't make me wait." Her rose up above her, blocking the light, as he had that one other night they'd shared.

She pulled him down to her, taking him in, crying out in wonder as he filled her. She looked up at him, into his beautiful eyes. And she felt him pulsing into her. She smiled, feeling powerful, triumphant. And totally free.

He relaxed on top of her. And then he rolled to the side, taking her with him, so they lay facing each other. She felt him start to pull away.

"No. Don't go...." She wrapped her top leg over his hip, holding him inside.

He chuckled then, and pushed himself against her. Oh, she did like that, to feel his body joined with hers.

For a time, they just lay there. She put her hand against his hard chest, felt his heart beating strongly, slowing a little as the minutes went by.

He touched her hair, smoothing it out of her eyes. "You looked so pretty, with all those little flowers in your hair."

"Umm...."

"Now all your little flowers are crushed."

She kissed his square chin. "Yes. So sad. My hair's a mess."

"I was too fast," he confessed ruefully, tucking her head beneath the chin she'd just kissed.

She snuggled up. "It's a wedding night. You can be fast if you want. And maybe slow later."

She could hear the smile in his voice when he asked, "Is that a hint?"

"I never give hints. I'm an up-front kind of girl."

"Oh, yeah?"

"Yeah."

"So tell me, how come you know so much about wedding nights?"

"I don't. I'm making it all up as I go along."

He pulled her closer. "You're doing a hell of a job."

"We've been over this. I'm a bright girl and I learn fast."

"Amen to that."

In one slow, lazy stroke, he ran his index finger down the side of her neck, into the curve where her collarbone started and then out over the rounded slope of her shoulder. She closed her eyes, enjoying the little sparks of sensation that his touch seemed to leave in its wake.

"Abby?"

"Umm?"

But he said no more. His hand continued on its teasing course, sliding over the outside of her arm. She kept her eyes closed. He touched each of her fingers, tracing them one by one. And then he pulled back from her a little. She sighed as she lost him. But her sigh turned to a gasp as she felt his hand there, at the secret heart of her, his fingers moving in the moistness and the heat.

"Cash?" Her breath came ragged. "Oh, Cash..."

And again, he said nothing. He let his caresses talk for him. Her body lifted; her thighs opened. Fulfillment washed over her in a warm, sweet wave.

Sometime later, as they lay side by side gazing up at the ceiling, she whispered, "Over the past couple of weeks, since I've known we would get married, I've started to wonder."

"About what?"

"About your bathroom."

Clearly puzzled, he repeated, "My bathroom."

"Your *private* bathroom."

"What about it?"

"Well, I've never seen it. All the times I've been in this house, I was never allowed in your private rooms."

"So?"

"So, I'll bet it has a big bathtub...."

He made a low sound in his throat.

She went on, "With whirlpool jets."

She felt him turn his head on the pillow. She turned her head, too, and their eyes met.

"Want to see it?" His straight white teeth flashed with his grin.

She nodded.

So he showed her his bathroom. They stayed there for quite a while, in the deep tub, enjoying those whirlpool jets.

Eventually, they went back to the bed, turned off the lights and snuggled beneath the covers.

Much later, Abby awoke to darkness and the warmth of her husband lying beside her. She reached out for Cash and felt him reaching for her. They made love again, in the dark, saying nothing, finding fulfillment at one and the same time.

Late the following afternoon, they drove to the Sheridan airport and took Cash's little Cessna to Mexico.

They stayed for a week, in an out-of-the-way place where the beaches sparkled like white sugar in the sun and the sky was the same clear blue as Cash's eyes. Cash had rented a small villa, with a red-tiled roof and pink walls and bougainvillea spilling over the fence that surrounded the pool and the back patio. They did nothing there but eat and sleep and swim and make love.

Next, Cash wanted to conduct a little business with some of his buddies in Cheyenne. So he took Abby along. She'd met most of them before, over the years. And she enjoyed seeing them again, from Chandler Parks, who lived in Phoenix and had recently married an Olympic volleyball star, to Redbone Deevers, who was an expert on the grain market.

Back in the eighties, when the FCC divided up the country for cellular phone franchises, Cash had bought the rights to a few remote areas. He was ready to unload them now. And Redbone knew a guy who knew a guy who wanted to buy areas for an independent cellular phone company that was just starting up. Abby sat in on most of their meetings, her head bent over the financial calculator she always carried with her, and kept track of the figures they threw around.

Cash had to put up with a little teasing about robbing the cradle and marrying "the kid," as they'd always called Abby. But it was good-natured teasing, and Abby thought he took it pretty well.

Of course they stayed in a luxury hotel. The bathtub in their suite was as deep and inviting as the one at home.

And it had whirlpool jets, too. So when Cash wasn't making deals, they spent their time in the bathtub. Or in the king-sized bed. Every once in a while, they ate at a nice restaurant. Or went dancing at a country-and-western club.

There in Cheyenne, they ran into one of Cash's ex-girlfriends. Abby recognized her immediately by how casual she tried to be when she said hello to him. She was a gorgeous woman. And she seemed nice. Abby could feel the effort she exerted to be cordial and to keep things light.

Cash, on the other hand, exerted no effort. He didn't need to. He smiled at the woman and asked how she was doing. He was friendly and charming. And when he walked away from her, she watched him go with hungry eyes—while he never looked back.

After meeting the ex-girlfriend, Abby couldn't help dwelling a little on the agreement she and Cash had made. A year of marriage, and that would be it. She could end up like the ex-girlfriend, staring after him every time she saw him, with longing in her heart. Unless both of them wanted it otherwise.

After their wedding night, after the week in Mexico, the agreement had come to seem unreal to her, something that had never actually taken place. But running into that old girlfriend brought the truth home to Abby: they *had* made the agreement. And it would have to be dealt with.

Eventually.

She was stretched out on the bed in their suite, thinking about the old girlfriend and her own foolishness in having proposed the agreement in the first place, when Cash returned from one of his meetings with the cellular phone franchise buyer.

He came and stood over her. "Okay, what's up?"

She gave him a distant smile. "Hmm?"

"What are you moping about?"

She closed her eyes and evaded his question by teasing, "Moping? Me?"

He dropped to his knees on the side of the bed and brought his face down to hers, so they were nose to nose. "Yes. Moping. You."

She wrapped her hand around the back of his neck. "I am not moping." And she wasn't, not anymore. She smoothed the hair at his nape.

He brushed his lips back and forth against hers.

"Kiss me," she said.

"I am."

"Those are just little kisses."

"You don't like little kisses?"

"I love them. But I want more. I want a long, deep, slow kiss."

He gave her what she wanted. And as he kissed her, he unbuttoned the blouse she wore. When all the buttons were undone, his lips left hers to burn a path over her chin and down her neck. He pushed the shirt open, out of his way. And he put his mouth on the swell of her breast, above her bra.

Abby moaned and clutched his golden head, pushing her breasts up at him, wanting him to suck them. With his index finger, he guided one cup of her bra out of the way. And then he took her nipple in his mouth.

She cried out. It felt so good, so right, so exactly what her body needed. What *she* needed: Cash. Loving her.

He joined her on the bed, and they helped each other to undress. He guided her to ride him. She took him inside her slowly, the way they both liked it done. And by the time she was rising and falling above him, she had no thought at all of old girlfriends or foolish agreements.

She thoroughly enjoyed the rest of their stay in Cheyenne.

But the best time of their honeymoon came at the end. When they got home to Medicine Creek, Abby admitted how much she sometimes missed the ranch. So they went out to the Rising Sun to stay for a while.

For four days, they rode out every morning early. It was the best time to ride, when the sun was just starting to rise, turning the sky to flame in the east. They rode side by side, their horses' hooves making dark trails in the dewy grass, grass that was turning dusty golden now, as the summer sun baked it brown. Abby loved the feel of the wind in her face; she loved riding into the cold shadows of the coulees and draws and then up into bright daylight on the high, windy ridges. She felt right inside herself to watch the light spread across the land as the sun rose, all the way to the Big Horns, making the snow on Cloud Peak reflect back, clean and pure and blindingly white.

Sometimes, they'd scare up an antelope or a jackrabbit. Their horses would shy, prancing sideways. And Cash and Abby would laugh together, as they had laughed together all the years of her life, and watch the spooked animal bound away, leaping with swift, sure economy through the golden grass.

Of course they'd make their rides useful, checking the ponds where the cattle gathered, seeing if any of the ponds had dried up too much. Cattle weren't terribly bright. They'd wade out into deep mud and get themselves stuck there, so Zach always tried to move them to a better water source before they got themselves in trouble in the mud.

After breakfast, sometimes Cash and Abby would head out with Zach and the hands, to cut hay or poison weeds or move the cows around. And sometimes they'd take off by themselves, to a secret place they'd always known of, on the banks of Crystal Creek, which ran in a lazy meander across much of the Rising Sun. There, in the shadows of the cottonwoods and willows, with the creek gurgling along nearby, they'd spread a blanket and share a picnic. Then later, since they couldn't keep their hands off each other, they'd make love with most of their clothes on, always ready to pull apart and button up if someone should chance to ride by.

They talked a lot about Ty, about the way he used to drive that old pickup of his up and down the ridges and draws of the Rising Sun as if there never had been such a thing as a road. They agreed that they missed him. That something had gone out of the world when he died. But they also agreed that it was almost possible to believe he'd never left them, when the sun shone on the Big Horns and when summer lightning forked across the sky.

It was a beautiful, perfect time. And Abby reveled in it. Her morning sickness had completely vanished. She felt fit and strong—and bonded to Cash in the most complete kind of way. She no longer yearned for the old days, when they had been mere comrades. Because now they were so much more to each other. She dared to hope that their marriage might turn out to be a lasting thing after all.

But then the notice about the University of Colorado's fall semester came in the mail, addressed to the ranch because that was the address Abby had given them the year before.

Abby tossed it in the trash basket in the front hall. And

Cash retrieved it. He came out on the porch to find her, slamming the screen behind him.

"You need this stuff, don't you?" He waved the papers at her.

She'd been feeling nice and comfortable, sipping lemonade, her boots up on the railing. She dropped them to the porch boards. "What stuff?"

"This stuff from C.U. It's got the day you're supposed to call, a tentative schedule and your PIN number so you can reregister."

She frowned at him, wondering what all that mattered. "But I'm not going back—not this semester, anyway."

His jaw hardened. "The hell you're not."

"But Cash…"

"What?"

"Think. It makes no sense for me to go back right now. The school's in Boulder. And Boulder's in *Colorado.*"

He made a snorting sound. "I know where Boulder is."

"Well, Cash. I'm pregnant."

"So?"

"So I'll be as big as a barn in a few months. I can't be off in Boulder—you know that."

"The baby isn't due till the end of January."

"January 20. That's the *middle* of January."

"Right. Fine. The semester ends before Christmas. And they always say first babies come late."

"*Who* says that?"

"Hell if I know. I heard it somewhere. Use your head, Abby. Your education matters. And you want to get as far along as you can. You could be within a semester of a four-year degree when the baby's born."

"Right. I could also end up having the baby in Boulder."

He frowned. Apparently, that idea gave him pause. But then he shook his head. "That's not going to happen."

"Have you told that to the baby?"

"Very funny."

"My doctor's here in Medicine Creek." She had started seeing Dr. Pruitt, at the Medicine Creek Clinic, the day after she and Cash had agreed to get married.

Cash waved that objection away. "So you'll have *two* doctors, one in Boulder and one here."

She stared at him, wondering what he could be thinking. Her education did mean a lot to her. But she would be *very* pregnant by the time finals came along; perhaps too pregnant to be going to school—let alone flying back and forth between Boulder and Medicine Creek.

And why was he suddenly so eager to send her away? Everything seemed to be going so well between them. Did he want to get rid of her?

Because she did not want to leave him. In fact, every day she spent with him, it became more clear to her that she actually *was* the marrying kind—as long as Cash was the husband in question.

The agreement came into her mind again. Why in the world had she ever suggested it?

She plunked her lemonade glass down on the railing. "Cash, come on. I could end up going into labor during finals."

"You won't."

"How do you know?"

He chuckled then. And he reached for her, wrapping an arm around her, drawing her close. She put her hands on his arms, resisting a little, refusing to meet his eyes.

"Come on, look at me," he coaxed. And he tipped up

her chin with a finger. "Hey. Think of it another way. You just might get through the whole semester. And that would put you one semester further along than you would be if you didn't give it a try."

She searched his eyes. She could see no hints of hidden agendas in them. But still, she couldn't help reminding him, "I thought we agreed to spend the whole year together. How can we do that if I'm off in Boulder and you're Lord knows where?"

"Ah." He looked smug. "You'd be lonesome without me."

She pushed at his arms a little. "Don't bet on it."

He pulled her closer. "Come on. Admit it. You can't stand to be away from me."

It was true. Too true. But she had no intention of admitting it.

He tipped up her chin again. "Kiss me."

"Cash..." She squirmed some more. But she kept her mouth tipped up so he had no trouble claiming a long, sweet kiss.

That night, back in the house in Medicine Creek after they'd made love, he promised her, "We won't be apart that much. I'll fly to Boulder every chance I get. And you can come home a lot. I'll *bring* you home. You want to be 'together' with me—you will be. Wait and see. But the baby coming is not going to interfere with your education any more than it absolutely has to, and that's that." He pulled her close, into the crook of his arm.

She snuggled against him and dared to whisper what was really on her mind. "Are you trying to get rid of me?"

He pulled her closer still. "Never. I swear it. I only want what's best for you."

He kissed her some more and then he made love to her again. While he was loving her, she believed him.

The next day, though, her own mother told her she was a complete fool.

"Your place is with your husband now," Edna said when Abby explained her plans. "You're a fool to leave him—and in your condition, too. It's irresponsible, totally irresponsible."

Abby spoke with all the patience she could muster. "Mother, Cash is the one insisting that I go."

They were having lunch together, in Edna's kitchen. Edna set down the sandwich she'd been nibbling on and announced stiffly, "I've noticed that when you want something, Abigail, you're not above pretending that everyone else wants it, too."

"Mother—"

"Please don't interrupt."

Abby sighed. "All right. What?"

Edna pushed her plate away and folded her hands on the table. "I'm going to be frank with you. Cash is a real catch. You're lucky you got him."

Abby held on to her temper by speaking with great care and precision. "I did not *get* him, Mother."

Edna waved a hand. "You know what I mean. He's a fine man, a man who could have had just about any woman. But he's always preferred the single life. Still, he did right by you, when another, lesser, man might not have. But he's only human. And if you leave him..."

"I'm not *leaving* him."

Edna sent darting glances around the bright kitchen, as if someone might be lurking nearby, listening in. Then she leaned forward and spoke low and intensely. "I'm just telling you that a woman has to look after her own interests. If she doesn't, take my word, there will be other women who won't hesitate to try to steal what's hers.''

Abby made a conscious effort not to roll her eyes. "Mother, you just said it yourself—women have always been after Cash. And if one of them was going to *steal* him, don't you think she would have done it by now?''

Edna clucked her tongue and sagely shook her head. "I'm only warning you. You could lose him.''

Just then Tess came in from the garage, where she'd been taking care of the laundry—separating the colors from whites, humming while she worked, Abby had no doubt.

Edna beamed at Tess. "Here's Tess. Let's talk about something more pleasant, why don't we?''

Abby was only too glad to oblige.

Cash and Abby flew to Boulder a few days after that. He wanted to get her all set up for the fall semester. They stayed in a nice hotel and ate at the best restaurants and looked through the want ads for just the right place.

The year before, Abby had lived with three roommates on the Hill, a few miles from campus, where most of the students who didn't live in the dorms found housing. The Hill consisted of an eclectic assortment of older houses, many of them run-down. Most of the frat and sorority houses were on the Hill, where keg parties went on almost nightly and stereos played into the wee hours. But in spite of the distractions and the noise level, a lot of the students who lived there worked hard and earned good grades. Abby had.

However, now she wanted her new husband to come and see her often. And Cash had grown a little beyond keg parties and Red Hot Chili Peppers playing all night long. Also, as her pregnancy progressed, Abby figured she would probably appreciate less hectic surroundings. So they chose a nice two-bedroom apartment far enough from campus that not many students lived in the area. As soon as they'd signed the rental agreement, Cash insisted that they go and buy furniture, linens and kitchenware. Then, while Abby was putting all the new things away, he went out and came back with a red Blazer.

"Cash, it's too much," she told him, when he pulled her out to her carport space to admire it.

"That Rabbit's on its last legs. I want you to have a dependable vehicle, one that's safe in the snow and on the mountain roads."

"Cash—"

He picked her up and swung her around. "Don't argue, Abby. Let me do this, please?"

She wrapped her arms around his neck as he slowly let her slide to the ground. "You've got to stop buying me things," she chided, rather breathlessly.

He kissed her nose. "No, I don't. You're my wife."

You're my wife. The words sang through her, causing such a burst of happiness that she did what he wanted, and said nothing more except, "Thank you," for the car.

He pressed himself against her. She felt how he wanted her, and wanted him right back.

"Come on," he whispered. "Let's go inside. Did you get the bed made?"

She shook her head.

"Hell. Who cares?" He grabbed her hand and towed her back inside and straight to the bedroom, where they fell across the brand-new bed. The mattress plastic crackled in protest beneath them.

They didn't care at all.

Once the apartment was all ready to live in, they returned to Medicine Creek. Cash went off to Cheyenne alone for a couple of days, while Abby stayed at home, helping Renata update the files on the office computer and driving up to Billings to choose the furniture and linens for the baby's room.

When Cash returned, he said he felt lucky. He would be thirty-seven the next day and he wanted to celebrate. They flew the Cessna to Vegas. There, they took in the shows and Abby played the slots, smiling, one hand on her softly rounded belly, as she thought of the little boy who'd tossed a quarter in a slot over thirty years ago and won ten thousand dollars when his mother's back was turned. Cash played poker with some buddies of his, two all-night games—one of them on his birthday. By the time he was ready to leave, he was just a little richer than when they'd gotten there.

Once again, they flew back home and then from home, they flew to Boulder. Cash stayed at the apartment for several days, while Abby got into her routine of classes and studying. Then he left; he had deals to make.

She missed him. And as soon as he was gone, her mother's dire admonitions returned to haunt her. She tried to keep her mind on her studies, but she just couldn't help wondering if her husband felt relieved to have some degree of his old freedom again.

On Friday, after he'd been gone for two days, she found herself sitting at her computer in the spare bedroom, trying to study. But her mind kept wandering. She kept thinking about how big she was getting. And wondering if perhaps Cash didn't find her very attractive. If maybe he...

With a grunt of disgust, she stood. Two days ago, before Cash had left, he'd made love to her at length, with enthusiasm. If he no longer found her attractive, he was one heck of an actor.

She just had to stop dwelling on the negative.

She needed some physical activity. Instead of sitting around stewing, she should get up and *move*. She could straighten up the apartment. It was starting to look just a little bit messy. In Medicine Creek, where they had a cook-housekeeper who came in five days a week, things always looked so neat and tidy. Cash had wanted to hire someone here. But Abby had vetoed that. It was only a two-bedroom place. Surely she could keep it up on her own.

She looked around her. "Ha!" she said to the books and clothes strewn everywhere. She should definitely do something about it.

But it was Friday night. She needed people, company—something to take her mind off her own silly doubts. She'd run into Melanie Ludlow, one of her roommates from last year, at the student union just yesterday. They'd spent a few minutes talking over old times. Melanie had congratulated Abby on her marriage and the coming baby, then she'd invited her to drop by the house anytime.

"Things are pretty much the same as last year," she'd said. "There's me, Sasha Thompkins, Libby Sands—and since we lost you, we got a friend of Libby's, Mandy Parks. Everybody would love to see you—and that rich cowboy of yours, too." Her roommates had all met Cash once or twice. "Well? What do you say?"

She'd promised Melanie that she'd call her. Real soon.

And now was as good a time as any. She picked up the phone and dialed the number of the house on the Hill where she'd lived the year before.

Melanie answered the phone on the first ring. Abby could hear music and voices in the background.

"How can you guys study with all that racket going on?" Abby asked.

"Abby. Hey. You coming on over?"

"Yeah. I think I will." Abby glanced at the clock on her desk as she hung up. A little after seven. She'd go over to the Hill for a couple of hours and enjoy the company. That should take the edge off of missing Cash so much. She'd be back home in bed by ten at the latest.

At seven-thirty, Cash pulled up in front of Abby's apartment building. He was grinning. She didn't expect him back until next week. But he'd missed her. And he had nothing to do that couldn't wait awhile. Tomorrow was Saturday. And Monday was Labor Day.

They could take off for the weekend—fly back home to Medicine Creek. Or maybe just drive over to Denver and stay someplace with decent room service and a big bathtub. He should have thought of it sooner.

Well, he had thought of it sooner. But they'd virtually been on one long honeymoon since the wedding. A holiday had seemed a little like overkill. And Abby had said she wanted to get some focus on her studies.

Hell, if she needed to work, that was all right with him. He could hang around, make sure she ate right, sleep next to her at night. He liked having her next to him when he slept, which bothered him a little. Made him feel dependent on her for his own peace of mind. He'd never in his life cared before if a woman spent the night or not.

But he supposed it was nothing to get his gut in knots over. They were married—for the time being, anyway. And married people slept together. No big deal.

He got out of the car, went around to the trunk and grabbed his suitcase. Then he jogged up the stretch of lawn and around the side walkway that led to the apartment's door. He reached for the handle and discovered it was locked at the same time as he really registered the fact that all the lights were off.

He got out his key and let himself in. "Abby?"

But he got no answer. The kitchen was right off the tiny entry hall. He reached in and flipped on the light, smiling indulgently as he saw that the remains of her last meal still sat on the table at the far end of the room. He glanced at the sink: full of dishes.

He picked up his suitcase and carried it to their bedroom. The bed wasn't made. He set down his suitcase with a sigh.

Chapter Eight

Melanie came running out when Abby pulled up in front of the slightly run-down two-story brick house with the broad, deep porch and the scraggly elm in the center of its patchy front lawn. "Nice wheels," she said.

"Thanks." Abby slid down from the driver's seat and walked around the front of the Blazer. As soon as she was out of the car, she could hear the music coming from the house.

"You are definitely looking ripe," Melanie declared. She was tiny, with big brown eyes and brown hair cut short.

"You mean fat, right?"

"No, I do not. You're not *that* big yet. Just kind of round and rosy. Your skin looks great and you sort of glow."

"I do?"

"You do." Melanie hooked her arm through Abby's. "Come on in. Party in progress."

By an hour after he'd arrived at the apartment, Cash had straightened the place up a little. And he was starting to wonder where the hell Abby could have gotten herself off to.

He found a can of cola in the refrigerator and took it into the living room. Dropping to the couch, he turned on the television. For a while, he just sat there, sipping his cola, switching from channel to channel. He watched a rerun of *Cops* for a while, hardly paying attention as two spousal abusers were towed off to jail and a major drug bust was accomplished with the aid of a battering ram.

By nine o'clock, he started getting worried. And not long after that, he started getting mad.

And then he saw himself for the moonstruck fool he was. Abby didn't know he was coming. She'd probably gone to spend the evening with one of her old girlfriends. She could be out until late—and there was no reason she shouldn't be.

He punched the "off" button and tossed the remote control on the couch. No sense sitting around here, waiting and wondering. He'd find himself a nice restaurant where he could get a strong drink and a thick steak. And maybe after that, he'd go cruising for a poker game.

Grabbing up his keys, he headed for the door.

"A woman never looks so beautiful as when she is with child!" the skinny guy in the black turtleneck shouted at Abby.

His name was Sven and he had backed her up against a wall of the living room about five minutes before. She wanted to escape him, but she felt a little sorry for him. So she just stood there, trying to look interested as he yelled in her ear in an effort to compete with Boyz II Men, which someone had turned up loud on the stereo.

Sven hollered, "There's such a deep, inner calm about a pregnant woman! Such a feeling of being in touch with the earth forces! Don't you think?"

Gamely, Abby attempted a reply. "Well, Sven, I don't know if I—"

He cut in loudly before she could finish. "I do believe I remember you! You lived here last year, didn't you?"

Abby nodded.

"Some kind of boring business-admin major, right?"

"Right," Abby replied. "With an emphasis in accounting and finance."

"Of course!" Sven looked down at her left hand, which was wrapped around a can of Sprite. Her diamond winked at him. "And now you're married!"

"Yes."

"Married!" Sven indulged in a chuckle. "How quaint!"

Abby gave him the kind of smile he deserved for a remark like that, and then took a sip of her Sprite. Right then, somebody had the good grace to turn down the stereo.

"Is your husband here?" Sven asked—more quietly, thank God.

She swallowed. "No."

Sasha Thompkins, on her way to the kitchen, paused long enough to lean in and inform Sven, "Give it up. She married a rich older guy. A total hunk."

"Ah," Sven said knowingly as Sasha moved on by.

Abby frowned. "Pardon me?"

Sven waved a skinny hand. "Nothing, nothing. It's just…predictable, that's all."

Abby wondered what had possessed her to feel sorry for him. "What's predictable?"

"Good-looking young women marrying older men with money. And having their babies. It's biology. What more is there to say?"

That did it. "How about, 'See you around, Sven'?" She ducked and tried to dodge beneath his arm.

He shifted his body slightly to keep her there. "I've offended you."

She leaned back against the wall and gave him a long, cool look. "Get out of my way."

Sven sighed. "How boring that you're angry." He leaned in close. "It is a simple fact that older, successful men look for young, healthy women of breeding age. Having made their mark on the world, they feel driven to propagate themselves. And there's no *blame* to it. The men can't help themselves, any more than young women can help being drawn to them, to the power and protection they represent."

"Goodbye." Abby moved faster that time, sliding beneath his arm, even shoving at him a little when he tried again to block her escape.

He called after her, "The truth hurts—I know it does!"

Abby set down her soda can on a scratched side table and kept walking. It was too smoky in the living room anyway, and now someone had put *Nirvana* on the stereo. She could do without Kurt Cobain. And she could use a little fresh air. She went through the hall to the kitchen, where Sasha was helping herself to a glass of white zinfandel from the wine box in the refrigerator.

"Abigail, Abigail." Sasha held up her full glass. "Where have you been?"

"Stuck in the living room with Sven."

Sasha burst out laughing. Then she blushed and covered her mouth with her hand. "Sorry, I'm a little plotzed. Love this white zin." She took a long drink, then looked straight at Abby, her expression suddenly severe. "But seriously. How have you been?"

"Great."

"You look…" Sasha waved her glass, seeking the right word.

Abby suggested, "Pregnant?"

Sasha gulped more wine. "Right on." She left the refrigerator and moved to Abby's side, where she lowered her voice to a conspiratorial level. "We've missed having you around." She drained her glass. "I know *I* have. You always minded your own business. And you never came up short when it was time to put in for the rent and the food." She brought a hand to her mouth again, this time to pat her lips, as if they'd grown numb. She frowned. "But then again, you *were* kind of a slob.…" She lifted her glass to drink some more, then stopped and looked into it, puzzled. "Uh-oh. All gone." Giggling to herself, she moved back to the refrigerator, where she pulled open the door and stuck her glass beneath the spigot of the wine box once again.

"God, Sasha." Libby Sands had appeared in the arch from the living room. "You better slow down."

Sasha straightened and shut the refrigerator. "I pay for my share." Defiantly, she raised her glass and drank long and deep.

With a sigh, Abby wandered on out the back door.

In the backyard, several guys from a fraternity house down the road had rolled out a keg. They sat around the lawn, drinking beer and talking about everything from obscure Danish philosophers to the Denver Broncos.

Abby sat on the back step for a few minutes, listening to their banter, appreciating the cool September night.

Then Melanie came out and found her. "Come on. Up to my room. We've hardly had a chance to talk."

Abby glanced at her watch. It was 9:35. "I should be—"

"Forget it. The night hasn't even begun. And your guy's in Vegas or something, right?"

"Cheyenne, probably."

"So there's no one waiting for you at home. You can stay for an hour or two. C'mon. Please?"

So Abby went upstairs with her friend. They sat on Melanie's bed together, the way they used to do. Melanie complained about her roommates a little, then told Abby all about the guy she'd met that summer, who'd turned out to be married and had broken her heart. And then she wanted to know about Cash and what it was like to be married—and having a baby.

Melanie asked gently, "You were pregnant at the end of spring semester, weren't you?"

Abby nodded.

"I knew it. I knew something was bothering you, big time. Something on top of losing your dad."

"It was...rough going there for a while."

"But everything worked out all right after all."

Abby thought about the agreement.

"Well," Melanie said, "didn't it?"

"Yes, it did," Abby said, sounding more sure than she'd been feeling the past couple of days.

"I gotta say, I admire you." Melanie widened those big eyes even more. "Your due date can't be too long after the end of the semester."

"January 20."

"Wow. That's cutting it close."

Abby nodded and tried to look self-assured. "If I don't make it, I don't make it. I'll take the semester over. But I wanted to give it a try."

"Well, your guy's really understanding to let you put so much focus on your education at the beginning of your marriage, with a baby on the way."

"He was the one who insisted I come here."

Melanie frowned. "Maybe he's trying to get rid of you."

Abby must have looked worried, because Melanie trilled out a laugh and poked her in the ribs.

"Not."

Abby made herself laugh, too.

Finally, at a little after eleven, Abby said she had to go. Melanie walked her out to the Blazer and told her not to be a stranger. Abby said she wouldn't, but as she drove away, she realized that it had been a polite lie. So much had changed in her life. She just didn't have a lot in common with her friends on the Hill anymore.

She knew that Cash was home the minute she walked in the front door and saw how neat everything was.

"Cash!" She ran to the bedroom and flicked on the light, sure she would find him lying right there on the bed, all rumpled and sleepy, waiting for her.

But the room was empty. She checked in the office room, just in case. No luck.

Back in the living area, she looked for a note. But he hadn't left one. She had no way to know if he would even come back that night.

She wandered back to her office, where she sank to the swivel chair at her desk and stared at her computer screen, feeling forlorn.

* * *

Cash returned at half past two the next morning. He parked in front of the building, then walked around back, to the carport. When he saw the red gleam of Abby's Blazer, right in her space where it belonged, he felt a sweet wash of relief.

An unpleasant, angry feeling swiftly followed. It was anger at himself, for skulking around back to look for her car instead of just heading straight for her door. And—unfairly, he knew—anger at her. Until this thing between him and Abby, Cash Bravo had never been a man who prowled around in the dark, checking to see if a woman's car was in its parking space or not.

A few moments later, Cash let himself in the dark apartment. Carefully, he shut the door behind him, putting his hand against it so that the latch wouldn't click too loud. He turned the dead bolt slowly so it wouldn't make a sound. Then he leaned against the wall and pulled off one of his boots.

He'd already decided to stretch out on the couch, instead of joining her in the bedroom. He told himself that he didn't want to disturb her.

But that wasn't the real reason. He wanted to feel casual about dropping in, not to make a big deal of it. But he didn't feel casual. He was bugged because she'd been gone when he showed up earlier.

And he didn't want to be bugged.

He didn't want to hold on to her too tightly. He didn't want to feel jealousy—or this hungry need for her. He wanted to go easy with this whole thing between them. He knew that was the right way to go.

Or at least, he knew it in his mind. The rest of him, however, seemed to have other ideas.

Cash pulled off his second boot and quietly set it on the floor beside the first one. Then, with a heavy exhalation of breath, he straightened and leaned against the wall.

He probably never should have let her talk him into making love on their wedding night. That night had set a precedent for all the nights to come. If he'd kept his hands off her, everything would have remained in perspective. He could have kept his mind on the real goal he'd had for this "marriage" of theirs: to provide for and protect both her and their child—period.

As for anything more, they could have taken it more slowly. They *should* have taken it more slowly.

But she wouldn't allow that.

And somehow, with him, Abby always got her way.

Cash closed his eyes, remembering....

Abby at seven, a streak of red dirt on her face and her hair in her eyes. "Cash. I'm big enough. I want my own horse." It was always a big deal for a ranch kid to graduate from some safe old nag to a green-broke horse you got to work into shape yourself. "Daddy says next year. You tell him I'm ready now. And I know the horse I want. She's a pretty little chestnut mare and she has a blaze on her forehead. Daddy got her last week at the wild-horse adoption over at the county fairgrounds."

"Listen, Pint-Size, if Ty says—"

She had grabbed his hand. Right now, more than fifteen years later, he could still feel that—her small, grubby paw in his.

"Come on, Cash. You tell him I should have that mare."

So Cash had found himself talking to Ty. And Abby had gotten her first horse.

"I'm coming to work for you," she had announced the summer she was sixteen.

He had grinned at her, thinking she was growing up

to be kind of cute, in a skinny-as-a-fence-post kind of way. "Abby, you should enjoy your summer. And if you really want to work, I'm sure Zach would let you—"

"I love the ranch, Cash. But I'm no rancher. I'm not like Zach. I'm like you, only with less of an instinct for bringing it in and more of a brain for the bottom line. That's why we're going to make a great team."

He'd had to stifle a grin. She was always so damn sure of herself, even when she didn't know what the hell she was talking about. "Look, if you need money for something specific—"

"I don't want you to *give* me any money, Cash. Forget that. I want a job."

"Well, you'll have to look somewhere other than my direction, Pint-Size."

"Do not call me 'Pint-Size.' I'm five foot six now. It's a perfectly respectable height."

"Sorry. But get real. I don't need anyone to work for me. I've got Renata in the office and she doesn't have enough to do as it is. She types a letter when I need it, and gets all the receipts together for the IRS boys when they insist on it. What are you going to do for me that I don't already get done?"

"I'll organize you. And you know I'm good with math. You know that computer you bought me? They have this program now, Lotus 1-2-3. You won't believe what it can do. You just have to know how to break it all down. Cash. I'm telling you. You need me. You need me bad...."

"Cash?"

He opened his eyes. She was standing in the tiny hall that led to the bedroom, a light on behind her. He saw her in silhouette, a shadow rimmed in gold. She wore one of those big T-shirts she liked to sleep in. It obscured the top of her. But he could see those long, smooth legs just fine.

"Cash!" She came flying at him. "You're back!"

She landed against him, and his arms wrapped around her all by themselves. He buried his face in her sweet-smelling hair, felt her soft thighs, the roundness of her belly with his baby in it, the fullness of her breasts.

She pulled back enough to kiss him, little pecking kisses all over his face. And while she kissed him, she babbled.

"I'm sorry I wasn't here. I didn't know you were coming. Oh, I have missed you." She wrinkled her nose a little. "You smell like cigarettes."

He wrapped his fingers in her hair, pulled her head back enough that their eyes could meet. "I had a few cigarettes, so what? I found me a friendly bar and got into a little game of five-card stud. A man can't play poker without a smoke or two."

She scrunched up her nose at him. "I thought you quit."

He tried to look innocent. "I did. I am."

"Yeah, right."

"Hey. If anyone should be able to do it, it's me."

She gave a little snort. "After all, you've had so much practice."

"Exactly."

They looked at each other. He still had his fingers twined in her hair. Her mouth looked so soft. He wanted to take it. So he was putting off taking it, just to prove to himself that he could.

She grinned, a naughty-girl grin. "I can feel that you're glad to see me."

Still holding her head so he could see her eyes, he rubbed himself against her, slowly, teasing both of them.

NO RISK, NO OBLIGATION TO BUY...NOW OR EVER!

GUARANTEED

PLAY "ROLL A DOUBLE" AND YOU GET FREE GIFTS! HERE'S HOW TO PLAY:

1. Peel off label from front cover. Place it in space provided at right. With a coin, carefully scratch off the silver dice. Then check the claim chart to see what we have for you – FOUR FREE BOOKS and a mystery gift – ALL YOURS! ALL FREE!

2. Send back this card and you'll receive brand-new Silhouette Special Edition® novels. These books have a cover price of $3.99 each, but they are yours to keep absolutely free.

3. There's no catch. You're under no obligation to buy anything. We charge nothing – ZERO – for your first shipment. And you don't have to make any minimum number of purchases – not even one!

4. The fact is thousands of readers enjoy receiving books by mail from the Silhouette Reader Service™. They like the convenience of home delivery...they like getting the best new novels BEFORE they're available in stores...and they love our discount prices!

5. We hope that after receiving your free books you'll want to remain a subscriber. But the choice is yours – to continue or cancel, any time at all! So why not take us up on our invitation, with no risk of any kind. You'll be glad you did!

THIS SURPRISE MYSTERY GIFT COULD BE YOURS __FREE__ WHEN YOU PLAY "ROLL A DOUBLE"

"ROLL A DOUBLE!"

place label here

SCRATCH HERE

SEE CLAIM CHART BELOW

235 CIS CDWJ
(U-SIL-SE-01/98)

YES! I have placed my label from the front cover into the space provided above and scratched off the silver dice. Please send me all the gifts for which I qualify. I understand that I am under no obligation to purchase any books, as explained on the back and on the opposite page.

NAME _____

ADDRESS _____ APT. _____

CITY _____ STATE _____ ZIP _____

CLAIM CHART

 **4 FREE BOOKS PLUS MYSTERY BONUS GIFT**

3 FREE BOOKS PLUS BONUS GIFT

2 FREE BOOKS   **CLAIM NO.37-829**

BUSINESS REPLY MAIL

FIRST-CLASS MAIL   PERMIT NO. 717   BUFFALO, NY

POSTAGE WILL BE PAID BY ADDRESSEE

SILHOUETTE READER SERVICE
3010 WALDEN AVE
PO BOX 1867
BUFFALO NY 14240-9952

NO POSTAGE
NECESSARY
IF MAILED
IN THE
UNITED STATES

Her eyes went dreamy. "Kiss me, Cash. Please?"

He wanted to ask her where she'd been, who she'd been with, what they'd done. But he refused to act like the jealous fool he knew he was.

"Cash?" A note of uneasiness had crept into her voice. "Is something wrong?"

"Not a damn thing."

"Then why won't you kiss me?"

"I'll kiss you."

"When?"

"Now." And he lowered his mouth to hers.

As he kissed her, he put his hands on her hips and slowly pulled up that T-shirt. She had nothing on under it. He cupped her bottom and pulled her closer, tighter into him.

"Oh." She sighed against his mouth. "Oh, yes, yes, yes...."

He scooped her up and carried her toward the light at the end of the hall.

The next morning, when they were sitting at the table, eating oatmeal, Cash told Abby that he was hiring a woman to come in three times a week.

"And do what?" she asked, irritated by the suggestion.

"You know what."

She felt defensive—and so she attacked. "That's ridiculous. We don't need a maid for a two-bedroom apartment."

"We *shouldn't* need a maid for a two-bedroom apartment."

She set down her spoon and took three deep breaths. "I'll do better."

He looked pained. "Abby, it doesn't mean a damn

thing to me if you can keep a house or not. I just don't want to walk into a pigpen every time I show up here.''

That hurt. Probably because her own idea of a real woman was someone who kept a nice house. She knew for certain that there were a lot of women out there just dying for their chance to pick up after Cash Bravo.

''Abby, are you listening?''

''Yes. And I understand.''

''You say that, and then you leave your junk everywhere. I don't want to live like that.''

''I know. It's a…problem I have. I understand why I do it, I swear.''

His brows drew together. ''Why?''

''Rebellion.''

''Against who?''

''My mother. You know how she is. The perfect homemaker. And I'm not her. I don't want to be her.''

''Fine. So you're all grown up now, right? You don't have to get even with Edna anymore. Get over it.''

''I'm trying.''

He looked doubtful. ''Abby…''

''What?''

''Maybe you just don't give a hoot about picking up your junk. I don't like to pick up after myself, either. So I hire people to do it. *They* make money. And *I* get to live comfortably. Everybody wins.''

He had a point, and she knew it. But still some frugal, self-sufficient part of her hated to admit that she was a hopeless slob who couldn't be bothered to put her own clothes away—let alone that she wouldn't do for Cash what a *real* woman would be eager to do. ''I just want to try, Cash. Please. Let me try. It just seems wrong to need a maid for a place this size.''

He sighed.

And she knew he would give her another chance. She smiled. "Thanks. I'll do better."

"Eat your damn oatmeal."

Obediently, she picked up her spoon and dipped it into her bowl.

And in the weeks that followed, Abby's housekeeping did improve slightly—enough to keep Cash from actually going out and hiring that maid.

Cash kept his promise and came to see her often. Sometimes he stayed at the apartment for days at a stretch. He was passionate and attentive. He went with her to the doctor and they signed up for a childbirth class, which took place on Wednesday nights in October and November. He promised to knock himself out to be there, and he did. In the six weeks of classes, he only missed two.

Twice, over weekends, they flew home to Medicine Creek. And two other weekends they drove in to Denver and spent Friday and Saturday night in one of the best hotels in town. The first weekend they spent in Denver, they dined at the Brown Palace and saw Dwight Yoakam live.

The second weekend, they ate at the Brown Palace again on Friday night. On Saturday, they tried a new Italian place.

"Right this way," the maître d' said. He led them to a nice corner table and promised that the wine steward would be right with them.

As the maître d' left them, Cash opened his menu and pretended to read it. But he was really watching Abby. He'd been having a ball with her the past several weeks, spending every available moment with her, giving in, really, to his craving to be near her. She seemed to want it that way. And besides, that had been part of their agreement when they'd decided to marry: to be together as much as they could.

She glanced up from her menu and their gazes locked. She grinned. He grinned back. She went back to deciding what to order. He went on looking at her.

He liked looking at her, studying the various parts of her. Right now, he was watching her hands as they held the menu. They were slender hands and she kept the nails trimmed short. Pretty hands, but useful-looking, too. And clean. He smiled to himself. Edna might have failed in her efforts to turn her only daughter into a happy little homemaker, but at least she'd won out when it came to personal hygiene. The grubby urchin of yesterday existed only in Cash's fond memories now.

"Abby? Is that you?"

Cash glanced up, frowning. A handsome, dark-haired kid hovered by Abby's chair.

Abby looked up from the tasseled menu and smiled. "Tony! Tony Ellerby. How are you?"

"Fine. I can't believe this."

Cash watched Tony Ellerby. The kid was trying not to stare at Abby's stomach. But he'd put two and two together, all right. Cash watched the kid, thinking that he was just about Abby's age, wondering how Abby knew him, what he might have been to her.

Tony asked, "Are you, uh, living here now? In Denver?"

"No, I'm still at C.U. We just came into town for the weekend." Abby looked at Cash, then back at Tony. "Tony, this is my husband, Cash."

Tony grinned. "Hey, how are you?"

Cash took Tony's outstretched hand, gave it a quick shake and then let it go.

Abby inquired, "What about you, Tony? I haven't seen you around campus."

Tony forked a hand through his thick black hair and explained that he was taking a break for a semester or two. Getting his "priorities" in order, trying to figure out what he really wanted from life. Abby laughed and said it was good to see him and she wished him luck, whatever he did.

"Old friend?" Cash asked casually, after Tony had said goodbye and walked away.

Abby nodded at him over the top of her menu. "We dated a couple of times last year."

Cash looked at his own menu. Then the wine steward appeared. Cash ordered wine for himself.

Abby waited for the wine steward to leave. Then she said quietly, "It was nothing serious between me and Tony."

Cash continued to study his menu, scanning the pasta selections, considering the veal entrées. "You never mentioned him, that I remember."

"We just had dinner once, and went to a show another time. No big deal."

Cash believed her. He knew her that well. If it had been a big deal between her and Tony Ellerby, he would have heard about it.

What bothered him had nothing to do with how many dates Abby and Tony Ellerby had shared. It had to do with the way his gut had knotted at the sight of that kid bending over his wife. With the possessive streak he'd discovered in himself. Never in his life had Cash felt possessive about a woman. Until Abby.

And then there was the guilt. Guilt that he was the one sitting across from her now, her belly so big with the child he had put there. As much as he hated the thought of her with anyone else, he knew that she should be sitting across from someone like Tony Ellerby tonight. It was the time of her life for casual dates with guys her own age, guys who would take her home later to that shabby brick house she used to live in last year with a bunch of other college girls. Instead, she went home with a husband fifteen years older than she was. And very soon, she'd be dealing with motherhood.

"Cash..."

He felt her foot, under the table, rubbing his leg.

He looked at her over the top of the menu. "Put your shoe back on."

"Are you jealous?"

"Do you know what you want?"

She picked up her water glass and sipped from it. Provocatively. "Oh, I do." Under the table, her toes trailed up and down his pant leg. "I know just what I want."

"Good. Because the waiter's coming."

She kept on stroking his leg with her toes all through the process of placing their order. By the time the waiter walked away, Cash's jealousy and guilt had taken a back seat to lust.

He didn't know how she did it. She was due to have the baby in just two months—and she was sexy as hell. Sometimes, he tried to control himself, worrying that all the lovemaking might hurt her or the baby. But she would remind him that the baby was fine, that the doctor said it was okay as long as she wanted to and he wanted to.

And they both did want to. All the time.

He shifted in his seat, coughing, trying to readjust for his arousal without being obvious.

Across from him, Abby grinned like a Cheshire cat. She knew exactly what she'd done to him. And she was proud of herself. He slid a hand down and captured her ankle.

"Oh!" she said.

He grinned right back at her. "Something wrong?"

She batted her eyelashes. "No. Not a thing, honestly."

"Good." He scooted his chair under the table a little farther—and then he put her foot on top of his thigh.

It took concentration; her big belly got in the way, but she managed to scoot closer, to put those naughty little toes right up against the part of him that was straining at the front of his pants. He tried not to gasp.

She went on grinning. He glanced around. People nibbled their antipasti and chewed their veal piccata and chatted casually between sips of wine. No one seemed to notice what the pretty pregnant lady was doing to her husband under the long white tablecloth.

Just then, the wine steward appeared with the bottle Cash had ordered. He uncorked it with a flourish, then poured a small amount for Cash to sample. Cash took a sip, then nodded. The wine steward filled his glass and left.

Cash raised his glass to Abby, as under the table she continued to drive him out of his mind. He knocked back a long sip, then set the glass down a little more firmly than necessary. "Are we going to eat?"

She looked rueful and adorable. "Well. I do keep thinking about that tub in our suite. It's so nice and big and deep."

"Fine." He pushed back his chair and threw a handful of bills on the table. "We're gone."

Abby took a minute to slide on her shoe and push back her chair. And then they were heading for the door.

"Is there a problem?" the maître d' inquired as they

fled past the reservation podium. He glanced at Abby's belly. "Signora, are you all right?"

"She just needs a little rest," Cash said.

"But—"

"I left enough to cover our meal on the table." Cash kept walking, pushing Abby slightly ahead of him.

The maître d' kept sputtering. "But, wait. Are you—?"

Abby gave him a smile over her shoulder as Cash pushed her out the door. "I'll be fine. Honestly. I just need a long, hot bath."

A couple of hours later, they lay together on the big bed in their suite, Abby on her side in a nest of pillows and Cash wrapped around her, spoon-fashion. He had his hand on her belly, feeling for kicks. He smiled. "A good one."

She gave a little mock groan. "I know—I felt it."

He nuzzled the back of her neck, breathed in the sweet scent of her. "I've been thinking."

She shifted a little, readjusting herself on the pillows, trying to get comfortable. It got harder and harder for her as the days went by.

"Abby? Did you hear me?"

"Umm-hmm. You've been thinking…"

"About next weekend…."

She groaned again, took his hand, kissed it and put it back on her belly. "Forget it. We're going home."

The next weekend was Thanksgiving. Abby wanted to go home to the ranch, where she'd spent every Thanksgiving of her life. Edna was planning a huge feast, to be prepared by the capable hands of Tess DeMarley.

"Abby, I don't think it's such a great idea for you to be flying now."

She put a hand over her ear—the one that wasn't buried in the pillow. "I can't hear you."

"Abby..."

She jerked away from him then and dragged herself to a sitting position, Indian-style. "We've been over this." She smoothed her big T-shirt over the heavy curve of her stomach. "I'll see the doctor Wednesday. If he gives permission—which he will, because I feel fine—then we are taking the Cessna home and we are having Thanksgiving the way we've always had it."

"But—"

"No. Listen. My mother drives me nuts. But I do love her. And she is expecting us. It will break her heart if we don't show up."

"Edna will understand."

"No. Edna will *say* that she understands. And inside, she'll be hurt. And anyway, you should have listened to me back in August when I told you I wasn't sure about getting in another semester."

"I know. I was a damn idiot."

"Well, fine. You were an idiot. But just because you talked me into coming here doesn't mean I'm giving up my Thanksgiving."

"I just didn't realize..."

"What?"

"How *big* a pregnant woman gets."

She sniffed and tried to act wounded. "Thank you very much."

"I mean it, Abby. We'll have a great Thanksgiving, the two of us. In Boulder, or here in Denver if you want to get away a little."

She dropped the wounded act and gave him that

straight-on, will-to-will look she had perfected over two decades of unremitting practice. ''We are going. And that's that.''

''No, Abby.'' He spoke firmly, to show her he could not be swayed on this. ''We're not.''

Chapter Nine

They flew back to Wyoming on Wednesday evening and spent the night at the house in Medicine Creek. Then, early in the morning, they drove out to the ranch in the Jeep Cherokee that Cash kept next to his Cadillac in the garage.

It was a cold, clear morning. Abby looked out the window of the Jeep at the rolling prairie land. To the east, from the higher points in the road, the fields seemed to go on forever, overlapping ridges and draws, rising to distant hills somewhere at the ends of the earth. But to the west, rising starkly, black and tipped with blinding white, the Big Horns loomed high, rough and proud, wreathed in feathery gray clouds.

Abby felt good for a woman who was as big as a cow, and pleased to be headed for her favorite place in the world. All the grass in the pasturelands had gone dusty brown months before. Abby watched it bend before a strong wind, rippling away toward the mountains. White patches of snow from a recent storm dotted the land, giving back a glare in the bright sun that made Abby squint. A line of fence ran along the ridge above the road and Abby spotted a sage grouse, scared from cover by some unseen predator. Its plump body rose from the ground in a flutter of gray wings, then dropped back to earth, bomberlike, not far from where it had taken flight.

She glanced at Cash. Sensing her eyes on him, he turned his head. He smiled, and she knew he'd forgiven her for keeping at him relentlessly until he gave in and brought her home.

Her mother came out of the house when they pulled up beneath the big Russian olive tree that grew in the center of the yard. The wind that had bent the brown grass of the prairie now whipped the skirt of Edna's Sunday-best wool dress around her legs. Abby felt satisfaction at the sight of her. She looked better each time Abby saw her, both stronger and happier, too. She was healing—from her illness and from the loss of Ty. Abby grinned to herself. Clearly, living with Tess DeMarley suited Edna—far better than living with her own daughter ever had.

Cash shoved open his door and headed for the porch. But Abby hung back, in the warmth of the Jeep, looking at the house, loving everything about it, from the shingles on the side-gabled roof to the four double-hung windows on the full-width front porch. Ross Bravo had built the house more than forty years ago, after a string of good years when beef prices had run high and the snowpack had measured deep. Before then, he and his wife, Matty, had lived in what was now the foreman's cottage, across the yard. Ross's daddy, the first John Bravo, had built the foreman's cottage sixty-five years past. Until then,

John, his wife, Belinda, and their son had lived in the small, dark homesteader's cabin. John's father, Matt, had built that cabin back when the Bravos had laid claim to the first acres that would become the Rising Sun. It still stood on the other side of the horse pasture, behind the barn.

On the porch, Cash and Edna waited for her. Abby got out of the Jeep and approached her mother with her arms out. Edna smiled and opened her own arms.

"Abigail," Edna said in her ear as they hugged—rather awkwardly, because of the size of Abby's stomach. "Oh, this is so good. To have you both home." Then she stood back. "My, my. You are getting..."

"Huge?" Abby supplied helpfully, and then shivered as a gust of frigid wind whipped around the corner of the porch and sliced right through her heavy sweater and pregnant-lady stirrup pants.

"Brrr," Edna said. "Let's get inside before we all freeze."

In the late afternoon, they sat down to the feast Tess had prepared. Zach had spent the morning out checking tubs—fifty-gallon barrels cut in half and filled with a molasses-based mineral mixture meant to supplement the cattle's diet of pasture grasses. He'd taken Tess's daughter, Jobeth, along with him. The six-year-old was pink cheeked and excited at having been included in the work of the ranch.

"Those tubs looked pretty good, don't you think, Zach?"

"Yep." He smiled at Jobeth. "Still pretty full."

She beamed down the table at him, worshipful, but restrained.

"This is wonderful, Tess," Edna said.

And it was. Abby looked up and down the long table in amazement. Even Edna, in her heyday, had never whipped up such a spread. The huge turkey was golden brown, and a steaming bowl of bread-and-chestnut stuffing sat beside it. The mashed potatoes looked as fluffy as clouds, the yams temptingly sweet under a drizzle of brown-sugar sauce. Tess had provided three kinds of green vegetables: steamed squash, peas and a broccoli casserole baked with cheese that set the mouth watering with its delicious scent. She had also set out two kinds of cranberry sauce, savory creamed onions, so many different pickled things that Abby couldn't count them all, a couple of yummy-looking gelatin molds and a tray of crudités, with the radishes cut to look like flowers and the carrots and celery all sliced at an attractive slant. Abby found it truly impressive, and regretted that in recent weeks the baby seemed to have pressed her stomach into a tiny corner beneath her ribs, leaving her appetite seriously impaired.

The two ranch hands, Tim Cally and Lolly Franzen, both murmured how good it all looked. It was Rising Sun tradition that the hands ate with the family on holidays if they didn't have somewhere else they wanted to go.

Cash took a bite of dressing. "Incredible," he said.

"I'm glad you like it," Tess replied.

Something in Tess's tone stopped Abby in the process of sampling the yams. Abby glanced at her mother's housemate. Tess was looking at Cash, a look that didn't last more than a split second. Cash himself hadn't seen it; his attention was on his plate.

But Abby saw it.

And knew what it meant.

It was the look Cash's old girlfriend had given him in Vegas. Yearning. Adoring. And hopeless.

Gentle Tess was in love with Cash. Abby set down her fork, what appetite she'd had a moment before suddenly fled. It was so obvious! How could she not have known before? Abby slanted another glance at Tess, who held out that wonderful broccoli casserole to Zach. Jealousy poked at Abby, a sharp, mean little jab. Tess was lovely, so slim and sweet—and so accomplished in all the womanly arts—arts in which Abby had absolutely no interest.

"I only wish Nate could have come, too," Edna said wistfully.

Cash laughed. "He'll be here for Christmas—just you watch."

"You think so?" Edna asked, brightening.

"Absolutely. Think back. He always makes it for either Thanksgiving or Christmas."

"Well, I wish he'd make it for both."

Cash shook his head. "If he showed up for both, we might get the idea he can't stay away."

Everybody laughed at that except Tess and her daughter, who hardly knew Nate.

Cash moved his thigh beneath the table so it brushed against Abby's. "Hey. You okay?" He indicated her untouched plate.

She gave him a smile. "You bet." And she picked up her fork and tackled the bread-and-chestnut stuffing.

Once they'd all sworn they couldn't eat another bite, Abby helped Tess clear the table and clean up the dishes. Then they played double-deck pinochle, Abby partnering up with Cash against Zach and Tess. Through the entire evening, Abby watched her husband closely.

By bedtime, she was positive he didn't have a clue about Tess's feelings for him. He treated Edna's housemate with the good-natured courtesy and warmth he'd always bestowed on the numberless women who had adored him over the years. And no one else seemed to notice what Abby had seen.

And really, as the evening had progressed, Abby began to suspect she might have only imagined that quick, worshipful glance of Tess's. Because after that single look, Abby caught no other hint that her mother's companion might be in love with Cash. Perhaps Abby was just being a paranoid pregnant lady and Tess DeMarley hadn't fallen for Cash at all—except in Abby's own jealous mind.

Besides, even if Tess *were* attracted to Abby's husband, she would never do anything about it. Because Tess DeMarley was every bit as exemplary a woman as everyone believed her to be.

And yet, lying in bed in one of the guest rooms later, listening to the wind whip and whistle around the eaves outside, Abby couldn't stop remembering the way Cash and Tess had laughed and talked together. And she couldn't help recalling her mother's warnings—and thinking of the agreement that still hung like a shadow over her relationship with Cash. If both of them didn't change their minds, in eight more months their marriage would end.

Every time she let herself think about that, she felt terrible.

Because she did not want her marriage to end.

Recently, she'd accepted the truth: she loved her husband—deeply and completely. As a woman loves a man.

She didn't know exactly how or when it had happened. Probably that night in the barn—maybe even before that. Lately, she'd begun to suspect that she'd been in love with Cash all her life.

But that night in the barn had marked the turning point. After that, she'd seen him as a man.

She'd run off to Boulder and then to Denver, trying to get away from what she felt. And then they'd decided to marry. And she'd starting letting herself get used to her love.

And now, finally, she could admit it to herself. She didn't want their marriage to end. She wanted him beside her in the night, across from her at the table, just plain nearby in general, for the rest of their lives.

"What is it?" Cash asked, out of the darkness beside her. "You keep wiggling around."

She felt a surge of her old independence, of irritation at him for having such power over her heart. "Sorry," she whispered sourly. "I'm just having a real adventure here, trying to sleep with this basketball in my stomach."

"Aw, poor baby."

He slid closer, fitting himself around her. The hair on his thighs scratched her a little; his hard hips cradled her soft ones. It felt good. So very good. With a finger, he guided a swatch of hair off her neck and put a kiss there.

"Feel better," he commanded.

She snuggled back against him, readjusting the pillow beneath her belly at the same time. "I do." It was true. Something happened when he cradled her at night. His body seemed to speak of peace to her body. And her body always listened. "Thanks."

"Any time." She felt his breath against her neck as he brushed one more gentle kiss there. "Go to sleep."

"I will."

And she did.

They stayed at the ranch through the weekend. It snowed on Saturday, wet snow, the white flakes whirling, making everything look hazy, turning to water the minute they touched down. Abby and Edna stood on the porch together and watched the clouds roll in overhead and the first wet flakes fall. Everyone else, including Jobeth, had gone out with Zach to help move some bred heifers to a pasture nearer the ranch buildings.

"They'll all be coming in wet," Edna said. She had on her coat, and she held her arms tight around her waist, shivering with each gust of icy wind that blew.

Abby pulled her heavy jacket closer, wrapping it snugly around the bulge of her belly. "They're having a ball."

"You wish you were with them."

"How did you guess?" Abby leaned from beneath the porch and caught a soggy snowflake on her tongue. It had melted almost before she felt its coldness. "But Cash wouldn't let me." She patted her stomach. "Too far along, he says." She leaned out once more, welcoming the wet flakes on her upturned face.

"He's right," Edna declared. "There will be time later for moving heifers on a snowy afternoon. And besides, I think it's lovely the way he cares for you, how much he loves you."

When she heard those words, Abby wanted to whirl on her mother and demand, He does love me? Are you sure? How do you know?

Somehow, she stopped herself. Questions like that would only get her more questions from her mother in return—worried questions, prying questions. Questions to which Abby had no answers anyway.

She needed to talk to Cash. To tell him she loved him. And to let him know that she, for one, wanted their marriage to last.

But right now at the ranch, with all the family around,

didn't seem like the right time. She decided to wait. Until they could really be alone, back in Boulder. She didn't want to think that it might go badly. But just in case it did, they wouldn't have the family to deal with, too.

"Let's go in," Edna suggested. "I'll make us some tea."

The kettle had started to whistle when they heard the horses and Zach's pickup in the yard. Abby ran out to meet them.

Cash's horse, Reno's Pride, a big gray gelding and a fine cutting horse, pranced to the side when she grabbed the bridle.

"Whoa, easy..." Cash soothed the horse. Then he leaned down and gave Abby a kiss. "Miss me?" he asked.

His lips felt icy against her own. She could smell the melted snow in his clothes and his breath made plumes in the cold air.

"Desperately," she told him, with just enough drama that he could think she was only playing.

Sunday morning, before they went downstairs, Cash actually tried to talk Abby out of returning to Boulder.

"Hey," she teased. "Remember? You were the guy who insisted I had to get in one more semester."

"That was insane of me. You should have had me locked up. I'm serious. We got back here safely enough. But let's not tempt fate. It can't be smart for you to fly now."

"The doctor said—"

"I know what the doctor said. And I don't care." He turned to the window and for a moment stood looking out at the gray day and the patches of sludgy snow on the roof of the barn. Then he turned back to her. "You can take the semester over again. Next year."

She was putting on one of the giant-sized tunic sweaters she wore all the time now. She smoothed it down over her maternity leggings and marched over to him in stocking feet, thinking of how she'd busted her butt in her investment and portfolio management course. And if she had to take the seminar in financial accounting again, she might just lose her mind. "No. Honestly, Cash. I really think I can get through finals before the baby comes. I feel good, I swear. And I've worked so hard...."

He smoothed a hank of hair out of her eyes. "I know. But—"

"No, really. I mean it. I want to finish out the semester. I really do."

He ran the back of his hand along her cheek and in his eyes she saw such tender concern.

I love you, she thought. The words sounded so sweet and soft in the back of her mind. She opened her mouth, almost said them....

But he spoke first. "I don't think it's safe."

She blinked. And remembered what he was trying to get her to do. "We are going. Today. I am finishing the semester, and that is that."

He sucked in a breath, then blew out his cheeks in frustration. "Abby, if you insist on going back, I think we should drive."

"Four hundred miles? Excuse me. I *will* go into premature labor if you put me through that right now." She placed a hand on his shoulder. "Look. We'll fly this one last time. And then, before Christmas, when we come home for good, we'll drive. How's that?"

He looked at her steadily. "If we're going there, we stay there. Until the baby's born."

She smiled at him, a coaxing smile. No way she was staying in Boulder for Christmas. But they didn't have to go into that right then. "Let's not worry about that now."

"Abby..."

"Cash..."

They glared at each other. And then they both laughed. He put an arm around her and pulled her close, so her big stomach bumped against him. Then he kissed her nose. "All right. I don't like it, but all right."

She smoothed the hair at his temples, thinking how she loved the little grooves that appeared in his cheeks when he smiled. Masculine dimples, that's what they were. But he would not have appreciated her pointing them out. So she didn't.

"I could shoot myself," he said softly, "for pushing you to go back in the first place. I don't know what the hell I was using for brains at the time."

He looked so worried. And so sweet.

Again, she almost said it: I love you, Cash.

But then she heard footsteps, out in the upper hall, and remembered her plan to tell him when they were really alone, when she didn't have to worry about dealing with anyone else. Best to stick with the plan.

They went down to breakfast a few minutes later. And a few hours after that, they were on their way to Sheridan to get the Cessna.

More than once during the flight, Abby started to tell Cash how she felt about him. But somehow, the words never found their way out her mouth. She told herself that she'd be foolish to tell him something so important while he was trying to fly a plane.

In Denver, it had snowed, too. And a lot of it had stayed on the ground. Abby looked out the window of the Blazer at the soft blanket of white and thought of

Christmas, which would be coming up before they knew it.

At the apartment, Cash carried their suitcases in. Abby headed straight for the thermostat to heat the place up, and from there to the bathroom. It was a funny thing about being pregnant. You spent the first three months bending over the commode, and the last three sitting on it.

"Do you want to go out to eat?" Cash asked, when she emerged from the bathroom.

She felt tired from the trip. But still, she wanted to say yes. Abby loved to eat out. It always seemed festive to her—plus, when you ate out, you got fed without having to cook or clean. In Abby's perfect world, people would either eat out or eat at the houses of other people who actually *enjoyed* cooking and cleaning.

People like Tess—who might or might not be in love with Abby's husband, but, in any case, was exactly the kind of woman most men wanted for their wives.

"Abby?" Cash was frowning at her. "You in there?"

She shook herself. "Uh, yeah. And let's not go out. I'll just whip something up, why don't I?"

He stared at her. "Are you feeling all right?"

"What do you mean?"

"I could have sworn you just said you'd rather cook something yourself than eat out."

"That's exactly what I said." She turned for the kitchen. "Sit down and relax. I'll call you when it's ready."

She found linguine and a can of clam sauce in the cupboard. And there was lettuce and a lone tomato in the crisper. And frozen Pepperidge Farm garlic bread in the freezer. So they had pasta, salad and bread.

It wasn't that difficult. And when they sat down to eat, the linguine was only slightly beyond al dente.

"Are you turning domestic on me?" Cash teased.

Even with Tess's feminine perfection taunting her, Abby wasn't willing to go that far. "It's the nesting instinct. It'll pass."

Later, as they were going to bed, she decided that the time had come to tell him. "Cash?"

He pulled back the covers and slid in beside her. "Yeah?" He canted up on an elbow to look at her, since she was sitting against the headboard.

"Well, I..."

And before she could say another word, a memory rose up to taunt her; a memory of something that had happened years ago.

It had been at a dance. A Fourth of July dance, out in Medicine Creek Park.

Abby could picture the bandstand, with loops of red, white and blue bunting tacked to the sides—and the dance floor, its railings draped in red, white and blue, as well. Overhead, the summer stars gleamed like sequins on a midnight blue gown. The weather had been warm and humid, unusual for Wyoming. Folks had remarked on the heat. Their faces had glistened with sweat when they danced.

And Abby had been eight years old.

She could almost see herself now, in blue jeans and pigtails, standing on the sidelines, clapping along to a Bob Wills song, watching her mom and dad as they danced....

Chapter Ten

The child, Abby, stood by the bandstand, watching her mother and father as they whirled around the floor.

She felt good watching them, because they were smiling at each other, smiles with love in them. Sometimes Abby could feel a coldness between her mother and father. She felt a coldness inside herself when that happened. A fear that her world, her life, might go bad somehow. That everything could change and there would be no one to love her and take care of her.

But at times like this, when her mom and dad looked at each other and something warm and private happened between them, Abby knew that her world was safe. She could smile and feel good and not worry about anything.

The band started playing another song, a faster one. Abby clapped her hands and stomped her feet as the dancers moved faster, up and down the floor, laughing and breathing hard, their faces shiny with sweat.

Abby looked around. Where was Cash? Cash would dance with her and it would be such fun. A few moments ago, she'd seen him dancing with Marianne Bowers, but now Marianne was dancing with Bart Crowley and Cash was nowhere to be seen.

Abby turned from the bandstand and the circle of light that glowed from the lanterns strung overhead. She took the trail that led down to the bank of Medicine Creek, which ran along one side of town and after which the town had been named. Down by the creek it was cooler, but moisture still made the air seem thick, as if you could taste it while you were breathing it. Frogs croaked in the darkness and the cottonwoods and willows grew thick and shadowy, hanging over the burbling stream and the trail. It was kind of creepy, but Abby could handle it. She could hear the music from the bandstand behind her. And if she looked back, she could see the gleam of the lanterns lighting up the night. She wouldn't get lost or anything, no danger of that.

Up ahead, she heard voices. She froze on the trail for a moment, listening. A man and a woman, she felt pretty sure. When she started walking again, she walked more carefully, trying not to snap any branches, not to make any noise. She was sneaking, really. And she probably shouldn't. But she did it anyway.

The voices stopped suddenly, but Abby knew where they had been coming from: a little picnic area on a clear spot above the trail. Abby slid in behind a clump of willows to see who it was.

She saw Nate and Meggie May Kane. Nate had come home again for one of his visits a few days before. He had a bandage on his hand, where the bull he'd ridden in the rodeo that day had stomped him. Nate liked to tempt fate by riding in the Powder River Roundup every year. That was what Abby's mom said. Just this morning, she had told him, "You just have to tempt fate, don't you, Nathan Bravo? You'll break your fool neck one of these days."

Nate was leaning against the picnic table in the middle of the clear spot. He had his arms around Meggie May and she was pressed up real close to him, closer than dancing, that was for sure. Their mouths were all mooshed up together in a kiss. A very *private* kind of kiss. One that went on for a long, long time. The white bandage on Nate's hand seemed to gleam in the darkness, like the lanterns back at the dance, as he held Meggie May so tight against him.

Abby knew she shouldn't be watching. But she just stayed crouched there, behind the willows, watching anyway.

Finally, Meggie May pulled back. She looked up at Nate. "I mean it, Nate. I love you. And I will always love you."

Nate took Meggie May by the arms. He pushed her back from him and stared down at her. "Give me a break," he said.

Abby could see his face pretty well. He had on his mean look, the look he gave people when he wanted to be safe from them.

"Nate." Meggie May sounded like she might start crying. "Please…"

"Look." Nate held Meggie May farther away than before. "If you want a good time, fine. But you shouldn't have followed me out here for anything else. Because you're never gonna get anything else from me."

Meggie didn't say anything for a minute after that. Abby discovered she was holding her breath. Very carefully, she let it out and then started breathing, real quiet, again.

Meggie stepped back. And Nate dropped his hands.

Meggie said, her voice all tight sounding, "I guess I always thought that if I told you, it would make a difference."

Nate made a disgusted noise in his throat. "Well, now you know. It doesn't make one damn bit of difference. Not to me, anyway."

Meggie started backing up, toward the slope that led down to the trail. She went past Abby's hiding place and took a few more steps backward. Then she whirled around and started running, off down the trail toward the lights and the music.

Abby turned back to watch Nate again. She thought he looked sad. He took a cigarette from the pocket of his shirt and lighted it, the match flaring, blinding Abby a little, so she closed her eyes. When she opened them again, Nate was just leaning there, against the picnic table, smoking.

Abby heard a sound on the trail. And Cash came out into the clear spot. Abby's heart lifted up high in her chest, in that happy feeling she always got at the sight of him. She almost leaped from her hiding place and grabbed him to come dance with her.

But then she realized that if she did that, Nate and Cash would both know she'd been spying and sneaking. So she stayed crouched in the willows.

"You seen Abby?" Cash asked. "Edna wants her."

Nate shook his head and blew out smoke.

Cash went over and hoisted himself onto the picnic table, a little ways from Nate, with his boots on the long bench. "Got a smoke?"

Nate gave him one and held up a match. This time Abby closed her eyes before it flared.

Cash blew out smoke. "Meggie May almost ran me down on the trail. She didn't look happy."

Nate grunted. "Am I gonna get a lecture here, Cousin?"

"She was crying."

"She's better off crying than if she'd stayed here with me. We both know that."

"Maybe you should give her a chance," Cash said.

Nate threw back his head and laughed a mean laugh. Then he turned so he was looking straight at Cash. "Don't give me advice, Cash. Not about getting serious over some woman, anyway. I'm never getting serious over a woman." Nate leaned closer to Cash. "And you understand that. Because even though you treat them so much nicer than I do, you're just like me. If some female wants to get rid of you, all she's gotta do is start sayin' how she loves you. And you will be gone."

Cash and Nate stared at each other, then Cash nodded. "You know, Cousin, you're brighter than you look."

Nate didn't say anything; he just went on smoking.

Cash got down from the table. He dropped his cigarette and crushed it with his boot. "Help me find the pint-size, will you, before Edna gets to worrying?"

"Sure." Nate ground out his cigarette, too. Then they went off down the trail together.

As soon as Abby was sure they were gone, she jumped up and ran the opposite way. She took the higher path, and she was back among the lights and the people a few minutes before the Bravo cousins got there.

Her mother got mad. "Where have you been, Abigail? I've been worried sick."

Abby lied and said she'd just walked on the high path

for a ways. But in her mind, she was remembering the lesson she'd learned.

She should never say "I love you" to Cash. Or he would go away.

"Abby?"

Cash was grinning up at her, still leaning on his elbow in their bed.

"Hmm?" She brought herself back to the present and put on a smile for him.

"What?" he asked.

She frowned.

He reached up and pulled on her hair, a teasing little tug. "You were going to say something?"

She couldn't do it. Not right now. She just could not do it. She shook her head. "No, it's nothing. Really. Nothing at all."

He put his hand on the hard mound of her belly, a possessive, tender gesture. She put her hand over his.

"Come on down here," he said. "Let's get some sleep."

She scrunched down and turned to her side. He helped her with her pillows and then he wrapped himself around her back.

"Are you all right?" he asked, after they'd lain there silent in the dark for a while.

"Sure. Why?"

"I don't know. You seem…"

She reached behind her and patted his hip. "I'm fine. G'night."

He pulled her closer. A few minutes later, she could tell by his breathing that he had dropped off. It took her considerably longer to get to sleep.

* * *

After that, it became a kind of game Abby played with herself. She knew she should tell Cash about her feelings, about wanting to make their temporary marriage a lifetime thing. But somehow, every time she was just about to do it, she found an excuse to back out.

And there were plenty of excuses to be had. Cash was forever leaving and coming back. He had his deals to make, but he seemed to want to be near her as much as possible as the time that the baby would be born approached. So she never knew, when she left for classes in the morning, whether he would be there or not when she returned. How could she plan a serious talk with him when she couldn't even be sure if he'd be there to listen to what she had to say?

Also, her end-of-semester workload kept her hopping. Finals seemed to be coming at her like a speeding train. And she kept thinking about Tess, the perfect woman, who just might be in love with Cash. So she expended more effort than usual in taking care of the apartment and keeping the refrigerator stocked. Plus, she wanted to Christmas-shop. And she did. She bought several gifts for her mother and Zach and Nate and that little girl of Tess's. And, of course, for Cash. Somehow, she managed to get them all wrapped, as well.

But something had to give. She ended up missing one of her scheduled visits to Dr. McClary, her Boulder ob-gyn. When she called and he fit her in two days later, he said her blood pressure was somewhat elevated. He made her stay for hours, to check it again and to run urine and blood tests. Then she had to come back the next day so he could tell her that her tests had turned out fine.

"Everything looks pretty good," he said. "We found nothing to worry about in the blood work. And no traces of protein in the urine, which might point to PIH. Are you familiar with that term?''

She nodded. ''I think they talked about it in our child-birth class. It's like toxemia, isn't it?''

''Pregnancy-induced hypertension. And yes, it is what we used to call toxemia or preeclampsia. Basically, it's late-pregnancy high blood pressure and it's nothing to fool around with. Right now, your blood pressure is within the safe range. But it's higher than it has been, and so it's something to watch. I think the best thing you could do at this point would be to reduce your salt intake as much as possible, get plenty of rest and carefully monitor your stress level. By that I mean, cut out anything that puts pressure on you.''

She gave him a look of great patience. ''I'll be even more careful than I have been about salt. But as far as the rest of it, well, my finals are in one week.''

He shook his head. ''You are having a baby, Mrs. Bravo, and very soon now. I understand that you are young and strong and that you imagine you can handle anything. But maybe you should consider taking those finals at some later date.''

''In a pig's eye, Dr. McClary.''

He chuckled at that and then grew serious once more. ''Take it easy, please. I want that blood pressure back down nice and low again the next time I see you.''

''But this is my last visit,'' she reminded him. ''Remember? I'll be going home in a week and a half. I already have my next appointment scheduled with my doctor in Medicine Creek.''

Dr. McClary frowned. ''Where is this Medicine Creek, now?''

''Northern Wyoming.''

"That would be a very long trip for you at this point in your pregnancy."

"Dr. McClary, I am going home as soon as my finals are through, and that's that."

The doctor looked at her over the top of the half glasses he wore. "On your way out, check in with Annie at the reception desk to make an appointment for next week."

"But—"

"There's no harm in being too careful. When I see you then, we'll discuss your flight to Medicine Creek."

"But I'm not going to fly. My husband won't let me. We're driving. That should be safe, right?"

"Probably," he said grudgingly. "But I'd still like to see you before you go."

Abby restrained a sigh. Just what she needed—something else to do next week.

Dr. McClary was still talking. "Also, you have some swelling now, around your ankles especially. And that's normal. But you're to call me immediately if you get any swelling in the hands or face, blurred vision or headaches."

Abby promised that she would contact his office if any strange symptoms appeared. Then she went out and told the receptionist that she'd give her a call as soon as she had a chance to check her schedule for next week.

At home, Abby hit the books good and hard. Cash asked her how her visit to Dr. McClary had gone. She lifted her cheek for his kiss and muttered, "Fine," thinking that she had to remember to call and schedule that last appointment. Then she went back to her studying.

The next week, she took her finals. She felt she did well on them, though she wouldn't know for sure until she received her grades. By December 21, she was done with school. She went to the registrar's office and told them she wouldn't be back until next fall. They agreed to mail her a copy of her transcript as soon as the new grades were posted.

She and Cash were packing for the trip back home when Annie, Dr. McClary's receptionist, called. Abby remembered at that moment that she'd never made that last appointment. She apologized profusely and then asked Annie to reassure the doctor that she was fine and had an appointment scheduled with her Medicine Creek doctor on the twenty-sixth, just a few days away.

"I'll need to speak with the doctor before I let you go," Annie said. "Please hold."

Abby waited, then Dr. McClary came on the line. He asked her several questions and then, reasonably satisfied with the answers, instructed her to stop every hour on the trip home to rest and stretch her legs. Abby promised that she would.

She hung up and looked around at the apartment. There were boxes everywhere. When they left this time, they wouldn't be back. Cash had already made arrangements for the sale of the furniture. And the few things they wanted to keep that wouldn't fit in the Blazer would be shipped back to the house in Medicine Creek.

Though Abby wanted to go home, she felt a little sad about leaving. She'd enjoyed the life that she and Cash had shared in the apartment. It felt more like her own home than the big house in Medicine Creek. To her, that house always felt like Cash's house alone. True, she liked the house. She liked the design and the decor; she and Cash had similar tastes. But it wasn't *her* house, not in any way. Cash had built it and chosen the furnishings years before. He had a cook and housekeeper who kept the place ready for him whenever he wanted it. To Abby, in some ways, that house didn't seem much different from the hotels they had stayed in together.

Here, it was another story. Here, she'd chosen most of the furniture herself. And she'd done good work here on her studies. She'd even learned to cook a few simple dishes in the tiny kitchen—thanks to the inspiration provided by her silly jealousy of Tess DeMarley. In this apartment, she and Cash had really *lived* as a married couple. Remembering their lives together here, Abby could almost tell herself that their marriage was a secure, permanent thing.

Abby lowered herself to the sofa, groaning a little at the effort it took her now to do something so simple as sitting down. Just as she got settled, Cash appeared from the bedroom, carrying a packing box. He lugged it over to the door and left it there to take out to the Blazer when the time came to load up. When he turned for the bedroom again, he smiled at Abby—a tender smile. Then he came over to her and dropped down next to her, stretching his arm along the back of the sofa behind her. With a sigh, she leaned her head into his shoulder.

"Tired?" He rested his head against hers.

"A little." She found herself thinking about the agreement. She never had managed to make herself talk to him about it. And she did want to deal with it, to tell him that she longed for nothing more than to put it behind them and stay his wife for the rest of their lives.

Her heart beat a little faster. Maybe now would be a good time. Today. Before they went home, while they were still here in this apartment where things had been so good between them.

He took her hand, turned it over and traced a heart in the center of her palm. "Who was that?"

"Hmm?"

"Just now, on the phone?"

"Dr. McClary's office."

He traced the heart again.

She knew he was waiting for her to tell him what the doctor had said. Reluctantly, she admitted, "Dr. McClary wanted to see me once more before we left. But it's all been so crazy I forgot to schedule an appointment."

"So when are you going in?"

"I'm not. There's no time."

"Abby..."

"No, listen. It's not a problem. He asked me a few questions, then said it was all right if I waited until Tuesday and saw Dr. Pruitt."

"Questions about what?"

She explained about her blood pressure. "But it's no big deal. He did a thousand tests on me last week and everything was fine."

"You're sure?"

"I'm sure."

He gave her shoulder a squeeze. "So you'll see Dr. Pruitt on Tuesday?"

She raised a hand, palm out. "I do solemnly swear."

"Okay."

He kissed the crown of her head. In a second, he would get up, go back to the bedroom, pack another box. Her opportunity, once again, would have passed her by.

"Cash?"

"Yeah?"

"Do you, um, ever think about the agreement we made before we got married?"

His body seemed to stiffen a little next to her. But maybe that was only her overactive imagination. He didn't pull away or take his arm from around her shoulders.

After a moment, he said, "The agreement we made?"

She had no idea how to read that. Had he forgotten about the agreement? Or was he simply stonewalling her?

She clarified. "You know, the agreement that we'd get divorced in a year unless—"

He cut her off. "I remember." He definitely did move back then, pulling his arm from around her and putting a few inches between them on the sofa. "What about it?"

"Well, how do you feel about it? Now, I mean? We've been married for a while. Do you still feel the same?"

His eyes gave nothing away. "If you want to talk about the agreement, Abby, maybe you should start with how *you* feel."

She stared at him, knowing he was right. And irritated at him, too. He just couldn't make this easy on her. Oh, no. He had to make her do it all.

Abby felt too antsy to remain seated. Grunting a little, she pushed herself to her feet. She went over to the glass door that looked out on a central courtyard. It was a gray day. Shrinking patches of snow sat on the tops of the hedges and on the grass, as well.

"Abby?"

She made herself face him. "I'd like to forget it, that's all."

"Forget it?"

What was the matter with him? He knew what they were talking about.

She spoke with exaggerated patience. "Yes. I'd like to forget the agreement. I'd like to go on from here as if we'd never made any bargain at all. I'd like to stay married come July."

He was sitting forward on the couch, watching her. But

she couldn't read his look. She had no idea what he might be thinking.

"Well?" she demanded after about a half a century had elapsed without him saying a single word. "I told you what *I* think. What about what *you* think?"

He stood. "Abby…"

She wrapped her arms around her huge belly and hugged herself, feeling lost and ungainly. And faintly nauseated. Her stomach ached suddenly, a dull, inflamed kind of pain. Dr. McClary had been right. All the stress had started to catch up with her. She made herself breathe deeply and told herself she would not feel angry at Cash because he was behaving just as she'd feared he would behave if she dared to broach this subject with him.

He approached her cautiously. She watched him come through wary eyes. Gently, he reached for her. She let him pull her close, her anger draining off a little in the comfort of his embrace.

"I think we should wait to decide on this."

She leaned her head against his shoulder. "Wait for what?"

"Until after the baby's born and you're more yourself."

She pulled back and scoffed, "Oh, please. I may look like I swallowed a watermelon, but I'm still the same person I've always been. I'm not going to be any more *me* after the baby's born."

"I think you know what I mean. You're eight months pregnant."

"So? My brain still functions. I still know what I want."

"I'd just rather wait to make any permanent decisions, that's all. Until the baby's born and you're absolutely sure of how you feel."

"I *am* sure. I just told you that. If there's anyone who's not sure here, it isn't me." She stepped back then, out of the circle of his arms.

"Abby, don't get all worked up."

The baby chose that moment to kick against her ribs. "Ow!" She grabbed her side.

"Abby..." He reached for her again.

And she let him gather her close. "I'm fine." She leaned into his embrace. "I just got a little boot in the ribs from you know who, that's all." She turned so his arms encircled her from behind. Then she took his hand and put it where he could feel the movement.

He chuckled. "Whoa, there. The kid's got a wicked punch."

"Yeah. Tell him to stop it."

Cash said nothing, only tenderly rubbed the spot. Abby allowed her body to relax more fully against him. Her stomachache and the feeling of nausea faded.

After rocking her lazily for a moment, Cash kissed her neck. Then he whispered in her ear. "Why don't you sit down and put your feet up for a while? I'll get back to packing things up."

In spite of his tender tone, she knew what he was telling her: the conversation was over.

And nothing had changed.

Abby felt drained. She looked around at all the open packing boxes, most of them still waiting to be filled. There was so much to do. Lately, there was always so much to do.

She murmured wearily, "I should be helping."

"Just rest for a little while. Please."

She let him lead her back to the sofa, where he propped her up against the armrest, with two pillows at her back and her legs stretched out along the cushions. "Comfortable?" he asked.

She nodded.

He kissed her on the nose and returned to the bedroom. Abby settled back among the pillows, trying not to feel sad. And trying not to let herself think that her husband had no desire at all to make their marriage last.

Chapter Eleven

They left for home the next day, early in the morning.

To Abby, the drive seemed interminable. Her back ached a little and the baby kept moving, poking her from the inside every time she just about got comfortable. Cash was wonderful the whole way, saying nice things to her while she muttered complaints and squirmed against the pillow she'd used to cushion her lower back. He insisted they stop every hour on the hour so that she could go to the bathroom and move around a little.

She bore the stops with bad humor, though she knew they were good for her. She didn't want to stop. She just wanted to get there. For some reason, all of a sudden, her bladder had decided to give her a break. She had to go to the rest room only once during the entire trip.

They arrived in Medicine Creek late on Saturday afternoon. Mrs. Helm, the cook-housekeeper, had been warned of their arrival and had left homemade soup and bread for them to heat up. Abby had very little appetite. She ate a few spoonfuls of soup and then got ready for bed.

Cash called the ranch from the bedroom as soon as Abby was settled in among the pillows. After he'd talked briefly to Zach, he handed her the phone. Abby spoke with her mother, who had driven to the ranch with Tess and Jobeth the day before.

Edna sounded happy and excited at the prospect of the holiday. "Tess and Jobeth went out today to collect cedar boughs. We decorated every mantel and banister with them. They're so festive, and they really make the place feel like Christmas. And you should see the tree. It's beautiful, honey. Tess has done so much. She is amazing. She put up the tree yesterday, right after we got here. And you won't believe the menu for the dinner she's preparing Christmas Day."

"I can't wait," Abby said dryly.

"The Panklevys quit." Sandy and Bill Panklevy had hired on at the ranch not long after Edna became ill. Sandy had been filling Edna's shoes.

"What will Zach do?"

"He'll hire someone else, of course. And that Sandy wasn't worth yesterday's coffee grounds anyway. Did you see a sign of her at Thanksgiving? No, because she and Bill had to take a week's vacation, that's why. And she has not kept the place up, not at all. Tess has been cleaning and cleaning."

"Tell Zach he shouldn't take advantage of her."

"Don't worry. I did. Tess will be getting a nice little bonus in her Christmas stocking. And guess what? Nate arrived this afternoon."

Abby grinned. "Cash said that he would, remember?"

"Well, Cash was right. I just can't wait for you two

to get here. Then we'll all be together.'' A silence followed, then she added softly, ''Except for your father. Oh, I do wish he could be here with us.''

''Me, too.''

''But I'm finding that it's not as bad as I thought it would be, this first Christmas without him.''

''I'm glad.''

''How are *you* feeling?''

Not so great, Abby thought. ''Fine,'' she said.

''You've been pushing too hard, haven't you? I can tell by your voice. Honestly, what in the world possessed you to even attempt going to college at a time like this in your life? I don't understand it. I will never understand it.''

''Mom. It's finished now.''

''And you'll stay home, where you belong.''

''I will. I promise.'' At least until next fall, she added silently.

''Well,'' her mother said. ''Thank the Lord for small favors. And now that you're home, I can see to it that you get your rest.''

''I'm counting on you to do just that,'' Abby said with some irony.

The irony was lost on Edna. ''Good. After all, we're only a few blocks away from each other. And I'm feeling so much better lately. I can be with you whenever you need me.''

''Thanks, Mom.''

''Oh, well. What is a mother for?''

They spoke for a few more minutes and then Abby said she had to go.

''See you tomorrow,'' Edna chirped happily, and hung up.

Abby reached over and put the phone back in its cradle

on the nightstand. Then she kissed Cash and snuggled down for sleep.

She felt better in the morning, though Cash said her face looked puffy. She remembered Dr. McClary's warning and considered calling Dr. Pruitt, even though it was Sunday—and Christmas Eve, to boot. But she put it off until after breakfast, and it seemed to her that after she got up and moved around a little, her face looked just fine.

They reached the ranch at a little before eleven. Edna came out to greet them. At the sight of Abby, she frowned. "You look terrible."

"Gee, thanks, Mom."

"Your face seems swollen."

"I tried to tell her that," Cash said from the back of the Blazer, where he was hauling out their bags. "She says she feels fine."

"I do," Abby said.

"You've pushed yourself too hard," Edna insisted. "It's written all over you. Have you seen Dr. Pruitt?"

"We just got in yesterday."

"Well, you'll see him right away, won't you?"

"The day after tomorrow, I promise."

Edna put her arm around Abby. "You come inside this minute and lie down." She cast an accusatory glance at the gathering black clouds overhead. "It's freezing out here and it's going to snow."

"Mom, the weather isn't my fault."

"I know, I know. Come on. I don't want you out in this."

Abby went along willingly, glad to be home and rather enjoying having her mother fuss over her.

"We'll put you right to bed," Edna said once they got inside.

"No way."

"But—"

Cedar boughs decorated the long table in the front hall. Abby grinned in pleasure at the Christmasy scent of them. "I'll lie on the sofa."

"But I think you—"

"Mom," Abby said sternly.

Edna let out a huff of air. "Oh, all right. Have it your way."

"Thank you. I will." Nate appeared in the entrance to the formal living room, which they hardly ever used. Abby held out her arms. "Nathan, you're really here!"

He enfolded her in a big hug. "It's good to see you, Pint-Size. *All* of you." The baby chose that moment to kick. Nate jumped back and looked down at Abby's huge stomach. "What was that?"

Cash spoke from behind her, on his way toward the central stairway with their suitcases. "The next Muhammad Ali. How's it goin', Cousin?"

"Can't complain."

Edna pulled Abby into the great room and over to a long, fat flowered sofa beneath the windows on the north wall. "This makes into a bed. Isn't that convenient?"

"Forget it, Mom. I'll lie there, but it stays a sofa."

"You are so stubborn."

"I am not going to bed in the middle of the great room."

"All right, all right. Sit down, then. And put your feet up." Abby lowered herself to the sofa, then Edna knelt in front of her and slid off her shoes. "We'll just make you comfortable...."

The tall tree stood opposite the windows and the sofa.

A thousand ornaments, some of them generations old, winked at Abby from the green branches. Brightly wrapped gifts were piled knee-high around the base. "Oh, Mom, you were right. The tree looks fabulous."

"These ankles are swollen."

"Don't nag, Mom. Please?"

"All right, all right." Edna was arranging Abby the way she wanted her, with her feet along the cushions, her legs covered with an afghan and her back against a nest of pillows, when Tess came in through the central hall from the kitchen and breakfast room.

"Abby, how are you?"

Abby looked up into Tess's beautiful dark eyes. "Just fine. But Mom won't stop fussing over me."

"Isn't that what moms are for?"

"Oh, I suppose so." Abby looked at her mother, so busy tucking in the afghan and plumping pillows, fixing everything just so. When she glanced up, she saw that Tess was watching Edna, too. In Tess's face, Abby saw humor and affection. Perhaps even love.

Tess looked up, and into Abby's eyes once more. Abby had the strangest feeling right then. A *sisterly* sort of feeling.

Tess grinned at her, a conspiratorial grin.

Abby couldn't help it. Even if the woman *was* perfect and possibly in love with Cash, Abby liked her. A lot.

"How about a cup of tea?" Tess suggested.

"You twisted my arm."

"Is it decaffeinated?" Edna asked anxiously. "She doesn't need any caffeine. Just look at her."

"Decaffeinated tea," Tess said. "Coming right up." She turned back toward the hall just as Cash came down the stairs. "Cash," she said. "It's good to see you."

Cash gave her a hug, then stepped back. "Merry Christmas."

"Yes, Merry Christmas."

"Where's Jobeth?"

"Where do you think? Out with Zach, probably pulling a calf out of a ditch or something equally exciting."

Cash laughed. "A born rancher, that kid."

"I do believe so."

Abby watched this innocuous exchange with eagle eyes—and couldn't drum up a shred of suspicion. Tess and Cash smiled at each other like old friends and nothing more. Cash turned for the front door to go and bring in the Christmas presents, while Tess continued on toward the kitchen.

Not too much later, Zach and Jobeth appeared, half-frozen and splattered with mud.

"We pulled a bull out of a ditch," Jobeth announced proudly.

Tess, who'd just come in with Abby's tea, couldn't resist a knowing laugh.

"What's so funny?"

"Nothing, nothing…"

"That bull didn't seem too grateful," Jobeth added. "He tried to kick Zach."

"He was just being a bull," Zach said.

"You. Bath. Now," Tess said to her daughter.

Jobeth scrunched up her nose, but headed for the stairs.

"I suppose you expect me to clean up, too," Zach said.

Tess looked him up and down. "It certainly wouldn't hurt."

"I'm going, I'm going," Zach said. He turned and followed Jobeth up the stairs.

Abby watched Zach go, remembering how Cash had

brushed aside her suggestion that Zach and Tess might get together. Cash was just too cynical; Tess and Zach would make a perfect couple.

Outside, it had started to snow. Abby watched the flakes whirl and dance beyond the window, coming down harder as each moment passed. "It looks like a mean one out there."

"But we're in here, all safe and warm," Edna said contentedly from over by the old stereo, where she was thumbing through the records. "Ah. Bing Crosby. 'White Christmas.' Just what I was looking for." She put the record on the turntable and Christmas music filled the air.

The snow kept up all the rest of that day, so everyone stayed inside, drinking hot cider, playing board games and visiting. Tess laid out a lunch of chili and corn bread that Nate said was the best he'd ever tasted. For dinner, Tess served them a savory venison stew.

In spite of the wonderful food, Abby couldn't drum up much of an appetite. Edna chided her for not eating. Tess asked if maybe she'd like soup or something lighter.

"Will you two stop fussing over me?" Abby complained. She felt just a little agitated, uncomfortable in her own skin.

Edna clucked her tongue and tucked the afghan around Abby's legs again. Tess went off to get more tea.

Again, Abby went to bed early. She was sure that by tomorrow, with another good night's rest, she would feel just fine.

But instead, she awoke in the middle of the night with an aching belly and a pounding head.

Abby groaned and pushed the covers down. It was too hot in the bed. And her skin felt so strange, all itchy and prickly.

She turned to her other side, moaning a little in the process, hoping the change in position might soothe her headache and make her stomach stop hurting.

"Abby, what is it?" Cash asked out of the darkness beside her.

She knew at that moment that she would throw up. She shoved back the covers the rest of the way and wind-milled her feet, groping her way out of the bed.

"Abby?"

Her feet found the soft bedside rug. With an agonized moan, she pushed herself to a standing position and headed for the bathroom, which was two doors away.

"Abby…"

She heard him jump from the bed, but she didn't dare turn to him or open her mouth to answer. Pressing her lips together, willing the nausea down, she shuffled along, one hand under her stomach for support. As soon as she made it into the hall, she used her other hand to drag the wall. That kept her from falling down—and helped her to find the way through the dark. The pain in her stomach doubled her over, though her distended belly didn't give her much room to bend.

At last, she came to the door of the bathroom. The white porcelain of the commode glowed at her fuzzily through the dark. She shuffled toward it.

"Abby?"

She waved a hand behind her, the best she could do for him right then.

"Let me help you." And his strong arms were there, supporting her, guiding her down over the basin.

What little she'd eaten came up. Cash held her shoulders, kept her hair out of the way.

When it was over, she didn't feel much better.

Cash found a washcloth on the edge of the sink. He ran water on it, wrung it out and then stroked it gently over her face. It felt cool. "Abby, my God," he whispered as he rubbed the cool cloth on her too-hot skin. "What's going on? You're burning up."

She leaned back against the side of the bathtub, panting, her stomach still aching and her head pounding evilly. "Something's wrong. I..." She closed her eyes, moaned, clutched her aching belly.

"Abby?"

She forced her eyes open, wanting to see him, to look at his beloved face in the soft glow from the night-light next to the sink counter. He knelt before her, holding that soothing washcloth. She could make out the shape of him. But he didn't look right. He looked...

Her belly cramped again. "Cash. I...my stomach. Hurts so bad."

"Are you in labor?"

"No. Not like that. It's really my stomach, not...the baby. And my head. My head aches like the devil. My whole body feels awful, all itchy and...bad...."

"All right. I'll call emergency. Get you some help." He started to stand.

She reached out and grabbed his arm, thinking of the storm outside, wondering where that help would come from. "Cash. There's more."

"God, Abby. What?"

"Everything's blurry. I...can't see very well."

"Cash? Abby?"

It was Tess's voice, coming from the doorway that led out to the hall.

"What's happened?"

She must have flicked on the light, because all of a sudden, the room seemed to explode into brightness.

"Turn it off!" Abby cried in a torn whisper that echoed in her head like a shout. "It hurts! Turn it off now!"

The room plunged back into blessed darkness once more.

Cash said, "Tess. Help us. She's vomiting. Her vision's blurry."

"And my head. It hurts so much...."

"I'll call emergency," Tess said.

Abby heard the soft thuds of her slippered feet running down the hall. She held on to Cash. "What about the storm? We'll never get out."

"Shh." He rocked her, held her so close, against his heart. "You'll be all right. I swear to you. You will be fine."

She pushed at him. Even the comfort he offered caused her pain. "Oh, Cash. The baby. The poor baby...."

"Shh. Quiet. Breathe. Relax."

She tried to listen to him, but she was so terrified. "Dr. McClary said I had to watch my blood pressure. He talked about toxemia. About how I should be careful."

"Toxemia? You never said anything about that."

"I know, I know. There was so much going on. And my blood pressure wasn't that high. I was sure it was nothing. Oh, Cash, what if—"

"Shh. I mean it. Breathe slowly. And relax."

It seemed like an eternity before Tess came back. But at last, she appeared again, a fuzzy shape in the doorway.

"They said the storm's broken up enough that they can send out the helicopter. They said to make her comfortable until they can get here."

"How long?" Cash demanded.

"Within an hour, they said."

Abby closed her eyes, against her own blurry sight, against the pain inside her head, against her whole body, which seemed to imprison her, itching and aching and hot. To her, an hour sounded like forever. She pressed her hand against her belly, where her innocent baby slept.

"Hold on," she whispered fervently. "Just hold on. For an hour...."

Chapter Twelve

Cash and Tess brought Abby downstairs to the great room to wait for help. They made her as comfortable as possible on the big sofa, which they opened up to a bed.

Nate and Zach appeared just as Tess had finished putting on fresh sheets and Cash was helping Abby to lie down. As yet, Edna and Jobeth remained in their rooms. Cash hoped to keep it that way, though he knew that was probably impossible.

"What's going on?" Zach asked quietly.

Tess calmly explained what had happened.

They all tried to keep their voices down, not only in the hope that Edna and Jobeth wouldn't wake, but also because loud noises hurt Abby's ears.

"They're ringing," Abby fretted. "My ears are ringing...."

Only one lamp burned in the room, turned down very low, since bright light caused her real pain. Tess tried to get her to drink a little warm broth, but Abby swore she would throw up again if she tried to get anything down.

A few minutes after they got her settled on the sofa bed, she had some kind of seizure. Her body flailed and twitched. It took all four of them to keep her from hurting herself. Finally, after what seemed a grim eternity to Cash, the seizure passed.

Soon after that, Abby got the dry heaves. When that was over, she slumped to the pillows, weak and feverish, hardly able to open her eyes.

Cash bathed her forehead with a cool cloth. Her lashes fluttered open. She forced a wan smile. "Cash?"

"I'm here."

"Kinda messed up, didn't I?"

"Shh. No, you didn't. You didn't mess up. Not one damn bit."

He was the one who'd messed up. From the first. He'd taken her innocence and put a baby inside her. And then he'd insisted that she go back to college. He'd seen himself as so damn noble, doing that. Making sure she got on with her education, in spite of what he'd done to her. Not even thinking that there was only so much one smart, scrappy woman could take. He'd ordered her to push herself. And so she had pushed herself.

And now, she would die for it. The way his mother had died all those years ago having his baby sister, who had died, as well.

"Cash?"

He looked down at her, hating himself, wishing only that there were some way he could switch places with her.

She whispered, "You're...good husband. Want you to know...love you...."

"God, Abby...."

"Just tell me...do you love me, too?"

It wasn't a big enough word for what he felt. Not by a long shot. Still, if she wanted to hear it, he would give it to her. "I do, Abby. I love you...." He couldn't be sure if she heard him. Her eyelids fluttered shut as he started to say it. She didn't open them again.

Tess put her hand on his shoulder. "You should get dressed. So you'll be ready when they come."

"Watch her."

"I will."

He flew up the stairs, yanked off the pajama bottoms he slept in and pulled on jeans, socks, boots and a sweater. Then he ran back down.

"Is she...?"

Tess put a finger to her lips. "She's resting."

He sat down on the edge of the mattress. Tess handed him the cloth she'd just dipped in cool water. He bathed his wife's hot forehead—and listened so hard for the sound of a helicopter outside that his ears hurt.

Twenty minutes later, they heard the beating of the blades as the copter set down out in the yard. Abby went into convulsions again just as Tess was letting the two EMTs in the front door.

Cash, Zach and the EMTs surrounded her. "Hold her gently, very gently," one of the EMTs said evenly as he pressed an oxygen mask over her face. "Just keep her from hurting herself. That's what we want to do now."

The other EMT expertly drew fluid from a vial into a hypodermic syringe. "Hold her arm," he said to Zach. "Hold it absolutely still."

When the seizure finally passed, Abby lay unconscious. They took her blood pressure. If it had been high before, now it was dangerously low.

"We need to get her to the hospital in Billings right

away," one of the EMTs said. "It's a tertiary care center. They have the facilities there to deal with this."

Cash stared at Abby, who lay there so frighteningly still. He turned to the man who'd just spoken. "I'm going with you."

"You're the husband?"

"Yeah. I'm the husband."

The man studied Cash, then shrugged. "Normally, we don't allow it. But you'd be hours getting there through all the snow. You can ride up front with the pilot."

"Fine. Thanks," Cash said, then couldn't help adding, "she's out cold. Is she…okay?"

The second EMT, who'd just come in with the stretcher, muttered something about a coma.

Cash turned on him, grabbed him by his down jacket. The rolled-up stretcher clattered to the floor. "What the hell did you say?"

The first man shouted, "Stop!"

Cash froze, then let go of the second man's jacket.

The first man said, "Look. Now's not the time for explanations. Or for you to be losing it. It's our job to get this woman and her baby to the help she needs. Do you understand?"

"Yeah," Cash said, breathing deep. "Sorry."

"We can't take you if you'll be a problem."

"I won't. I swear it."

Edna chose that moment to appear from upstairs. "What is going on? Abby? Oh, no. Not my little girl…." She started for Abby.

Tess went right to her, embracing her—and, at the same time, keeping her from getting in the way. "It's all right. The helicopter's here. They're taking her to the hospital now."

"But what's happened?"

Tess led Edna to a chair. "Here. Sit down. I'll explain everything we know so far."

Cash realized he'd forgotten his wallet. Grateful that Tess was dealing with Edna, he ran up the stairs. He grabbed his wallet and a jacket. When he got back down to the main floor, they'd already taken Abby out to the helicopter.

"We'll get there as fast as we can," Nate promised.

"Fine," Cash said on his way out the door. "Look out for Edna."

"You know we will."

As it turned out, Cash found the helicopter flight the most bearable part of what followed. They were moving, at least, through the darkness, above the white, cold land. Moving fast toward the hospital where Abby could get help.

Things got unbearable pretty quickly once they got there. After filling out a ream of paperwork, Cash had to do what he hated doing: he waited. He drank machine coffee and sat. When he couldn't stand sitting, he paced. He realized later that the doctors had worked like demons and that he really hadn't waited that long at all—it only seemed like it.

Finally, a doctor came out and explained to him about Abby's condition: eclampsia, it was called.

"It's what we once called pregnancy-induced toxemia," the doctor said. "And nowadays, it's rare. Especially in a case like your wife's, where there's been adequate prenatal care, no indications of trouble during the pregnancy and no family history of high blood pressure. I will say that it occurs more often in young, first-time mothers, like your wife. And as has happened with your wife, it tends to strike very suddenly, in the last trimester.''

"How is she?"

"At this point, she remains unconscious, but stable.''

"The baby?"

"The baby seems fine.''

"Seems?"

"We've conducted an ultrasound. And a stress test. We have no indications of fetal distress.''

"And?"

"I understand that the pregnancy is thirty-six weeks along.''

"That's right.''

"How confident are you of that figure?''

"Very confident.''

"All right, then. At thirty-six weeks, the lungs are mature enough that the child should have no trouble surviving outside the womb. As you may have deduced, the only way to help your wife is to deliver the baby.''

"So deliver it. Deliver it now.''

"We intend to. However, your wife's body shows no signs of labor. Dilation and effacement are minimal. And we feel that to induce labor with the mother unconscious is not advisable.''

Cash remembered a word from those classes he'd gone to with Abby. "A C-section?''

"Yes. It's the wisest course in this case. And cesarean procedures are quite safe nowadays. An incision will be made in the lower abdomen, through to the uterus.''

Cash thought of them cutting into Abby and felt sick to his stomach. The doctor was still talking.

"The baby will be removed, and the incision closed up. Recovery takes a little longer than from a vaginal delivery, but for most women who have a cesarean, vaginal delivery of future babies is possible.''

Cash didn't give a damn about future deliveries. As far as he was concerned, there wouldn't be any of those. ''Fine. Do what you have to do.''

''Good enough.''

''When?''

''Immediately. We'll have some papers for you to sign and then we'll go ahead.''

''Get the papers.''

The doctor turned.

''Wait a minute.''

The doctor stopped, turned back. ''Yes?''

''She's in a...coma, isn't she?''

The doctor hesitated, then admitted, ''Yes. I'm afraid so.''

''You said she'd get better as soon as the baby's born. That means she'll wake up, right?''

''Yes. She should.''

''She *should?*''

''In most cases—''

''Just tell me. Will she wake up?''

The doctor sighed. ''The prognosis is good.''

''That means yes.''

''Yes. With reservations.''

''What reservations?''

''Mr. Bravo, there are no guarantees in a situation like this one.''

At first, they tried to tell him he couldn't be there for the operation. But he remembered what he'd learned in those childbirth classes. Fathers were often present during cesarean births.

"But the mother is not usually unconscious," the doctor argued.

"If she wakes up, she'll want me there."

"Mr. Bravo, she won't wake up. She'll be under a general anesthetic."

"A general anesthetic? But I thought—"

The doctor sighed. "We do often use spinal blocks when performing C-sections. But not in the case of eclampsia. Spinal blocks can lower blood pressure and your wife's blood pressure is too low already."

"Fine. Whatever. I want to be there. I *will* be there. I'll stay out of the way and I'll keep myself in hand."

In the end, they allowed it.

The surgery took place in a rectangular room, with the operating table in the center and bright lights above it. Cash saw a long table against one wall. And counters and sinks lining another wall. There was more, of course, much more: cabinets filled with equipment, machines and trays of instruments that Cash couldn't name.

Abby lay unmoving on the center table, draped in hospital green, hooked up to a number of machines that the surgery nurse explained would monitor her vital signs through the procedure. Several drapes hung from tracks on the ceiling, surrounding Abby's abdomen. There was a screen on wheels, which they placed at Abby's shoulder level. Cash stared at that screen, wondering what the hell it was for. And then he understood: as long as he didn't go around it, he wouldn't have to see what they were doing to her.

That was just fine with him. He'd stick with the top half of her. He'd promised to hold it together, and he would. But he could use all the help he could get.

He asked to be able to hold her hand. They said it would be okay. So he clutched her limp fingers in his rubber-gloved fist and prayed silently that she would be all right.

Once the anesthesiologist gave the go-ahead, the operation began. Cash stayed beside his wife, holding her hand, as the doctor on the other side of the screen described every move he made.

It didn't take that long. Cash heard a baby's cry.

"Look at those shoulders," the doctor said in satisfaction. "Mr. Bravo, you have a son."

Cash thought he'd sell his soul for a cigarette. "A son?" he repeated, as if the word were new to him.

"Yes," said the doctor. "A fine, healthy son."

Cash bent close to Abby and whispered through the mask they'd made him wear. "It's a boy. We have a little boy, and he's fine." He knew she couldn't hear him, but he didn't care.

Behind him, Cash could hear the baby crying. A nurse had carried him to the table against the side wall, where the process of examining, weighing and initial cleaning up took place. Through this, the baby cried louder than before. Cash clutched Abby's hand and told himself she would be okay as, on the other side of the screen, the doctor began the work of sewing her belly up again.

At last, after several minutes, the examining nurse confirmed the doctor's diagnosis: the baby was whole and sound.

"Would you like to hold him, Mr. Bravo?"

Cash laid Abby's hand gently down and turned.

The nurse held out a tiny, squalling red thing, which she'd already wrapped up to keep it warm.

"Just for a moment," she said.

Even though a mask covered her mouth, he could see her smile in the crinkles around her eyes.

Cash backed up a step, and came up short when he hit

the operating table on which Abby lay. He stared at the bundle in the nurse's arms.

And all at once he was fifteen again, and the tiny red thing was Abby. And Ty was there, grinning.

"Come on, hold this pint-size little thing. Don't you be shy, Cash. She won't break. She's gonna be a tough one—I can feel it in my bones. Tough, and beautiful, too. What more could a daddy ask for in his child?"

"Come on, Mr. Bravo," the nurse said. Cash could hear the warmth and humor in her voice. "Hold your baby. Here you go."

Cash opened his arms, hardly knowing now from then. And the nurse put the squalling bundle in them.

He looked into the wrinkled face. The crying stopped. And the blue eyes met his, so wise, so watchful.

"Tyler," Cash said, as the name came into his head. "For your grandpa on your mama's side. And Ross—for your great-grandpa on my side. Welcome to the world, Tyler Ross." Cash turned to Abby, grinning. "What do you think? Tyler Ross."

His grin quickly faded as he remembered that Abby couldn't hear him. She lay on that metal table, as still and quiet as the grave.

"A Christmas baby," the nurse murmured from behind him.

Cash looked up at the big institutional clock on the far wall. It was four in the morning. On Christmas Day.

He had a flash of the tree in the great room that Tess had decorated with such care. And all the presents under it. By the time he'd put the gifts he and Abby had brought under there, too, the presents had overflowed across the floor. Abby had bought so damn many, and insisted on wrapping every one herself.

"Christmas babies bring good luck," the nurse said.

Cash looked down at Abby once more. "I just hope to holy hell that you're right."

As soon as he left the operating room, Cash called the ranch. Zach answered. Cash gave his cousin the news and learned that Edna and Nate were on their way.

Eventually, when they had Abby settled into a room, they let him be with her. The room wasn't the same one that Edna had stayed in; it had a different number on the door. But it looked identical, with one tiny window, a white curtain that could be pulled around the bed and a single chair. The half bath, as in Edna's room, could be entered through a door about eight feet from the end of the bed.

Cash pulled up the chair so he could sit by the bed. He took his wife's slim hand and just looked at it. He thought about all the times he'd looked at it before, from when she was a baby and it had wrapped around his index finger, holding tight, through her childhood when it was always dirty and always grabbing for something she wasn't supposed to have.

More recently, he remembered that hand reaching up, pulling him down for a kiss. And holding that menu, in that Italian place in Denver, just before that kid her own age had walked in, confronting him with his own scary jealousy—and reminding him once more of all he had stolen from her: her youth, and her freedom....

God help him, let it not be her life, as well.

He closed his eyes, rubbed them. The room seemed lighter, somehow. He turned toward the window. Out there, dawn was breaking. But inside him, it seemed there was nothing but endless night.

He laid his head down on the bed, beside her. Still holding her hand, he closed his eyes.

"Cash?"

He lifted his head. Edna was smiling down at him. He raked a hand through his hair, rubbed the back of his neck. "Sorry. Must have dropped off...."

She put her hand on his shoulder. "Nate and I are here now. We'll sit with her. You go get some food into your stomach."

"No. I don't want to leave her."

"Go on. You have to eat. And you can come right back."

"Did they tell you about the baby?"

"We've already seen him." In spite of the worry lines between her brows, there was real joy in her voice. "My grandson is a fine-looking boy."

"I named him. Tyler Ross Bravo."

Edna's eyes filled. She had to bite her lower lip to tame the tears. "Perfect," she said.

Cash turned to Abby, where she lay so pale against the pillows. "Do you think she'll like that name?"

"She will love it."

"She hasn't woken up yet. She's supposed to wake up. Soon. If she moves or makes a sound—anything— we have to call the nurse right away."

"Go get some food and coffee," Nate said from where he stood by the door. "We'll watch while you're gone."

Cash knew they were right. He should eat, walk around a little, maybe look in on Tyler Ross. "All right." He stood, then he glanced at his watch: after nine. "How was the drive up here?"

"Don't ask," Nate replied grimly. "There are two new feet of snow on the ground. We made it. That's what matters."

Edna sank into the chair Cash had vacated, and took up the hand that he had set down.

"If she moves—" he began.

"Go," Nate said. "We're here. We'll look out for her."

Cash went to the cafeteria, where he drank two cups of coffee and forced down some eggs and toast. Then he visited a rest room, where he splashed cold water on his face, rinsed his mouth and combed his hair. After that, he made a stop at the nursery, where they let him hold Tyler Ross. He was back in Abby's room within half an hour of the time that he'd left.

"Any change?" he asked hopefully.

Edna just shook her head.

Nate had talked the nurses into getting them two more chairs. They settled in for the vigil.

It was a vigil that lasted eight more hours, hours that seemed like years to Cash.

Then, at five-thirty in the afternoon, Cash felt Abby's hand move in his. He looked at her face.

And her eyes slowly opened. "Cash?"

He squeezed her hand. "I'm here, Abby. I'm right here."

Chapter Thirteen

"They do say mother's milk is best," Edna remarked in a tone of loving disapproval.

They were sitting in the living room at Edna's house. Abby looked up from her son, who was sucking happily at his bottle. "Well, now, Mom. Tyler seems to like this bottle just fine."

"He'll be colicky. *You* were colicky, even though I kept you on the breast for a full year, just the way all the books said."

"Tyler's six weeks old now. Not a sign of colic."

"Sometimes it comes on late. And allergies. Bottle-fed babies always develop more allergies."

Tyler drained the bottle and let go of the nipple with a rude little pop. Then he burped loudly and his mouth stretched wide in what his mama chose to think of as a great big smile. Abby bent down and kissed him, then looked up at her own mother again. "You know, Mom, there's really no point in talking about this. Your grandson's a bottle-fed baby. That is not going to change.''

"Well, for the next one..."

Abby let out a groan. "Mom. Let's not start planning the next one yet, okay? I'm just getting used to this one." She smoothed a diaper on her shoulder, lifted Tyler Ross and gently set him there. After a moment or two of gentle pats, he burped again. "There," Abby said. "That's better, isn't it?"

Edna watched adoringly. "You astonish me."

"Why?"

"You're so relaxed. You're going to be a good mother."

"I'm *already* a good mother. And you don't have to act so surprised about it."

"Well, but you know how you always were. More interested in horses and math books than in dolls. And you always swore that being a homebody wasn't for you."

"I'm still not a homebody."

"You know what I mean. You swore you'd never get married and have children. But now here you are, a wife and mother. And you're just a natural with that baby. I don't know how you do it. I remember with you I could hardly enjoy myself. I was always nervous, trying to do everything right."

"Well, you know me. No chance of doing everything right anyway, so I might as well relax."

Edna actually chuckled. And then she frowned once more. "But I do worry, about our Tyler not getting all the benefits of breast feeding."

"Edna, stop it." Tess had appeared from the kitchen, carrying a coffee tray. "Tyler's doing just great. Look at him." She stared, dreamy eyed, at the baby in Abby's arms.

Abby let out another groan. "Tess, you've got that silly look on your face again."

"I can't stop myself. He's so adorable." Tess carried her coffee tray into the room and set it on the low table in front of the sofa. "Let me hold him."

Abby held out her son. Tess gathered him close. "Oh, he feels so good." She cooed and rocked the baby a little, then she grinned at Abby. "I always wanted about a hundred of these."

"Better get to work."

"Abigail," Edna chided.

Tess and Abby shared a laugh, then Tess sat on the end of the sofa and cuddled with Tyler, as Edna poured the coffee and passed it around.

"When is your six-week checkup?" Edna asked.

"Tomorrow, 9 a.m. sharp," Abby said with a little flutter of anticipation. She hoped to get a clean bill of health at last, because she had plans. For herself and Cash. Very intimate plans.

She and Cash needed a little intimacy. Lately, it seemed to Abby that he'd become somewhat distant with her. He'd been absolutely incredible through her illness. But in the past few weeks, since she'd been feeling so much better, he was forever on his way somewhere. He would make a point to help with Tyler, getting up for night feedings and even changing a diaper or two. But he never seemed to have much time to spend with Abby alone—except when both of them were sleeping.

Abby understood, of course. He had his business deals to catch up on, and though Tyler was easygoing for a newborn, he'd still managed to change their lives in a thousand ways.

Abby felt that what she and Cash needed was a good shot of romance. The married kind, in their bed. And in their whirlpool bath. And in a number of other locations she could think of without a great deal of effort.

All the books said that they could have romance right now—just not actual intercourse. But with Cash so preoccupied, Abby hadn't found the way to approach him about those other kinds of lovemaking. She felt more confident that she could bridge the distance between them if she knew they could just do whatever came naturally.

So she wanted that okay from Dr. Pruitt. She wanted it a lot.

"You've recovered so quickly," her mother said. "It's a miracle, really."

"Dr. Pruitt says that in cases like mine, as soon as the baby's delivered, the mother usually improves right away—as long as she received help in time, I mean."

"Oh, you were so fortunate."

"I know. I had Cash. And Tess." Abby looked at the woman across the coffee table, who was cooing and gurgling just like the baby. Tess stopped cooing long enough to give Abby an affectionate smile.

"Well," Edna said, "even if you feel better now, it's nothing to fool with."

"I'm not fooling with it, Mom. I promise. I'm taking good care of myself." She sat up straight and drew her shoulders back proudly. "This morning, my blood pressure was 120 over 60."

"That's good," Edna admitted.

"It's better than good. It's terrific. Now, if I can just get my stomach back in shape."

Tess glanced up again from gumming Tyler's fingers. "One thing at a time," she said.

"I started doing stomach crunches a week ago."

"Are you crazy?" Edna asked.

"No, I am not crazy." She thought about Cash. She did want to look good for him. "Just determined."

"To hurt yourself."

"I'm not hurting myself. I'm careful. Honest. I take it slow and steady." She lowered her voice and leaned toward her mother. "And I'll be the happiest woman alive when that creepy numbness around my incision goes away."

Edna sighed. "You're just like your father. Every time he broke a bone—and he broke a lot of bones, if you recall—he would start exercising the minute the cast was off. I still remember him sitting in the kitchen of the foreman's cottage, lifting a weight on a leg that he'd broken, tears running down his face. I told him, 'Ty, the way you work that thing, you'll break it all over again.' 'No, Edna,' he says to me. 'What I'll do is make it strong.'"

"He was something," Abby said reverently.

"He was crazy," Edna declared.

Tess said, "I think we need a clean diaper here." They all looked at Tyler, who gurgled and cooed, content with the world and his place in it.

The next morning, Abby left Dr. Pruitt's office with a big smile on her face. The doctor had told her just what she wanted to hear. She was ready once more to be a wife in every way.

Abby longed to share the good news with Cash. But she would have to wait, for a little while, anyway. Cash had flown to Vegas early the day before—for a big card game, Abby suspected, though he hadn't been specific about details when he said goodbye. He was due back tomorrow afternoon. And then she'd give him the good news. She'd do it the best way: up close and personal.

At home, Abby counseled with Mrs. Helm, the cook-housekeeper, for forty-five minutes. She was taking no chances on her own cooking tomorrow night. Once they'd settled on a special menu, Mrs. Helm went out to shop for groceries. Abby took Tyler to her mother's and then drove all the way to Billings to do a little shopping of her own. She bought a sexy cocktail dress and some lingerie that was black and slinky and not meant for any-one but a husband to see. Abby thought she looked pretty good in both the dress and the lingerie—considering she'd had a baby and nearly died six weeks before.

It was after dark by the time she got home, and it had also started snowing.

"What can you be thinking of, out driving in that?" Edna complained.

Abby soothed her mother, collected her baby and went home to the big house that always seemed so empty when Cash wasn't there. But she didn't feel quite as lost and forlorn as she'd felt on the other nights recently when Cash had been gone. She had tomorrow to look forward to, after all.

She awoke in the morning all jittery and eager. When Mrs. Helm came in, Abby asked her if she could stay a little later than usual to serve the dinner.

"It shouldn't be much after eight, I promise," Abby said. "And as soon as it's on the table, you could go ahead and leave. And if you want a few hours off during the day today in exchange, that would be fine. Or I'll pay you overtime. Whichever. It doesn't matter to me."

"Now, now, slow down," the kindly Mrs. Helm replied. "I'll be glad to stay. It's no problem. And I think I understand what you want. A beautiful table with tempting food—and a little privacy as soon as dinner is served.''

Abby beamed. ''Yes. That's it exactly. Mrs. Helm, you are an angel.''

''I'll just take myself out the back way, as soon as you two are enjoying your meal.''

''Oh, thank you. I can't tell you. I owe you. Big time.''

Abby decided that as much as she adored her son, she didn't want him interrupting anything on this special night. So she called her mother next.

Edna was not so kindly as Mrs. Helm. ''Abigail, what is going on? Yesterday, you drove to Billings in a snowstorm.''

''It had just started to snow when I got home, Mother.''

''And today, you want to drop your baby off with me again, this time for a whole night.''

''Is that a 'no,' then? Are you telling me you won't take Tyler for the night?''

''Of course I'm not telling you that.''

''Then what are you telling me?''

''I'm not telling. I'm asking. What is going on?''

Abby sighed. ''Oh, all right. I want an evening alone with Cash.''

After a silence, Edna murmured, ''Well. Why didn't you say so?''

''Does that mean that you'll look after Tyler?''

''I'd be pleased to, honey.''

Abby took Tyler to her mother's at three in the afternoon. Then she went home. At four, she sank into a scented bath from which she didn't emerge until five. Once she'd slathered lotion from head to toe and dabbed perfume at every pulse point, she dedicated an hour to fiddling with her hair and putting on her makeup. By the time she was all dressed in her sexy lingerie and new cocktail dress, it was after six—and Cash wasn't home yet.

Expecting him to walk in the door at any moment, Abby went out through the living room to the dining room, where she discovered that Mrs. Helm had outdone herself. The sight of the table made her sigh: a snowy lace tablecloth, gleaming silver and china, red roses in a cut-glass bowl and long cream-colored candles in crystal candle holders. Abby debated over whether to light the candles or not. She decided to wait until they sat down to eat.

She went to the kitchen. "Mrs. Helm, it's all just perfect." She sniffed the air, which carried the rich scent of Madeira-braised ham. "It smells like heaven in here."

Mrs. Helm turned to her. "And you look just beautiful. Mr. Bravo won't care about dinner at all once he sees you." Mrs. Helm held out a wooden spoon. "Here. Taste this."

Abby tasted. "Umm."

"More salt?"

"No. It's just right."

Abby wandered back into the dining room and then on into the living room. She put on a stack of romantic CDs and turned the lights down nice and low. Then she picked up a magazine and turned one of the lamps up a few notches so that she could read.

Half an hour later, she'd thumbed through the two *Western Horseman* magazines and the three *Architectural Digests* on the coffee table. She got up and went to the kitchen again.

"Everything okay in here?"

Mrs. Helm smiled. "Just fine."

"Good. Terrific." She ducked out of there and went

back to the living room, where yet another romantic CD was playing. She switched it off. All those strings were starting to get to her.

She went to the bedroom. The lights were low, the bedcovers turned invitingly back. Not a single article of her own clothing was strewn anywhere. All lay in readiness for the romance to come.

Only the husband was missing.

Fifteen minutes later, he called.

"Abby, I'm sorry. This is taking longer than I planned."

She could hear masculine laughter and glasses clinking in the background.

"I meant to call you earlier, but I couldn't break away."

"From what? A card game?"

"You guessed it." He sounded sheepish. "I'm on a roll. I can't quit now."

She wanted to scream at him, something shrill and hateful and totally unfair.

He asked carefully, "Abby, are you all right?"

She reminded herself that he hadn't known what she planned, that she shouldn't take her disappointment out on him. "I'm fine. When will you be home?"

"Tomorrow for certain."

Abby heard another man's voice, muffled, from his end of the line.

Then he said, "Listen, I have to go now."

She whispered, "Goodbye," but he was already gone.

She hung up very slowly. And then, for a few minutes, she just sat, her hands folded in her lap; she felt sad, disappointed and a little silly all at the same time. Finally, she dragged herself to her feet and went to the kitchen to tell Mrs. Helm that Mr. Bravo had been detained until tomorrow.

Mrs. Helm looked at her for a long moment. "Are you all right, then?"

She forced a smile. "I'm just fine."

"I'll clean things up, shall I?"

"Leave it all. Get it tomorrow."

"Let me just put the food away, then."

"Whatever you think." Abby turned to go, then stopped and turned back. "Thank you."

"You're very welcome, Mrs. Bravo."

"Just call me 'Abby.'"

Mrs. Helm promised that she would.

Abby leaned wearily on the door frame and slipped off her high-heeled shoes. Then, in stocking feet, she returned to the bedroom, where she took off her dress and her beautiful lingerie and put it all away. She washed her face and brushed her teeth.

As she climbed into the big bed alone, she couldn't help wishing that she had the nerve to go get Tyler from her mother's house. To hold his small, warm body would have been a great comfort right then. But that would only get Edna all stirred up, worrying that something was wrong.

And was it? Abby couldn't be sure. Cash was Cash, after all. He made his money gambling, whether it was poultry futures or five-card stud. She didn't expect him to show up at five-thirty every night. And she knew that, as his wife, there would be nights when she would sleep alone.

She didn't mind sleeping alone sometimes. As long as it didn't become a habit.

But her husband was a smart man. He'd read more than one book about childbirth and recovery. He'd gone through those childbirth classes with her. He knew what her six-week checkup meant. And he knew that it had taken place yesterday. She'd had it marked on the calendar since the day she got home from the hospital. And yet he'd chosen to be gone when she went in for it....

No, she had to stop thinking like this. Cash had no idea of her plans for a romantic evening. She had never told him. And she had no right to expect him to read her mind.

Still, she just couldn't shake the feeling that things weren't right between them. Things hadn't seemed right for a few weeks now.

She wanted to talk to him about it. But she didn't know quite how to broach the subject with him. And what would she say, anyway?

Are you avoiding me? Is something wrong? Are you tired of me? Are you just waiting for next July, when you can be free of me?

When she asked the questions to herself, they sounded weak and whiny. How would they sound like anything else to Cash?

And she couldn't stop thinking about the way he had reacted that other time, before they left Boulder, when she had tried to talk to him about their future as a couple. He'd made it painfully clear that he didn't want to discuss it.

Yet he had also promised that they could talk about it again after the baby came. So he had to be expecting to hear more on the subject.

Abby rolled over, punched her pillow, sighed aloud in the dark, lonely room. She just knew he wouldn't like it if she brought up the agreement again. She could feel it in her bones. Secretly, she feared that as soon as she brought it up again, she would lose him.

No. Actually, it was worse than that. In her deepest heart of hearts, she feared that she had already lost him.

At Christmas, before Tyler came, when she got so sick, she had told him that she loved him. So much else about that night was a scary blur to her now. But she remembered that moment, after the first set of convulsions had rattled through her body, when she had honestly feared she would die.

She had dared to whisper of her love. And then she had asked him if he loved her, too. He had hesitated, but then he had said it: "I do, Abby. I love you...."

She remembered his words exactly. It seemed they were engraved on her soul. Everything got fuzzy after that. She recalled no more until she woke up and learned that Tyler had been born.

But she *had* told Cash that she loved him.

And he had said that he loved her, too—which was true.

He had always loved her, *would* always love her.

But not the way she wanted to be loved. Not the way she loved him.

The past few weeks, she couldn't shake the growing conviction that the darkest fear of her childhood had come true.

She had told Cash she loved him.

And now he was going away.

Oh, he had stayed close during her illness. But now that she'd recovered, she would lose him. Because he just wasn't a marrying kind of man.

He'd given his son his name and he would see to it that his son's mother was well provided for. But other than that, he would want to be free.

And if she dared to try to talk to him about it, she would only lose him all the sooner.

Chapter Fourteen

Cash returned home the next day, as promised. But he'd hardly walked in the door before he told Abby he was heading out again—for San Francisco this time. He wanted to talk to some old buddy of his about investing in a new computer chip that hadn't been put on the market yet.

Carrying Tyler, Abby trailed after Cash into their bedroom. She stood in the doorway, holding their son, watching her husband as he emptied dirty clothes from his bags.

"Cash, you just got home." She tried to sound reasonable, and thought she succeeded pretty well. "I was hoping we could—"

"I'm sorry," he cut in without letting her finish. "But this could be a big one. They say this chip is a damn miracle. And if I miss out now, my chance won't come around again."

She said nothing for a few minutes. Cash moved back and forth between the bureau and the bed, collecting clean underwear and socks. Then she tried a different approach. "I know. How about if Tyler and I go with you? You know it always helps to have me there to keep track of the numbers. And Tyler may as well get used to our traveling life-style."

Cash tossed a stack of underwear in his suitcase and turned to her. "Abby, it's not a good idea."

"Why not?"

"You've been very sick."

"But I'm fine now. I saw Dr. Pruitt day before yesterday. For my six-week checkup, remember?"

He turned for the closet and disappeared inside. When he came out, he was carrying a stack of shirts, folded and wrapped in plastic from the dry cleaner's.

Abby stroked her son's small, warm head. "Dr. Pruitt says I'm fine. Completely recovered. In every way."

"Well, that's good." Cash set the shirts in the suitcase. "But you have the baby to think of."

"I *am* thinking of him. He's coming, too, remember?"

"Abby, he's too young to be dragged all over the place." Cash headed for the closet again.

She waited for him to emerge. When he did, carrying two pairs of slacks and two jackets, she reminded him, "Your mom and dad dragged *you* all over the place, almost from the day you were born."

He marched back to the bed and tucked the slacks and jackets into a garment bag. "Tyler's not going to have that kind of life."

"Why not?"

"It's not a good life for a kid."

"You loved it. I know you loved it. You used to tell me how you loved it!"

He looked up from the garment bag, frowning. "Quiet down."

On her shoulder, Tyler was squirming. She realized her voice had become a little shrill. She patted Tyler's back and forced a low tone. "You were a happy little kid, Cash. You know you were. It was only later, when your mother died and your dad took off without you, that you—"

"All right." His tone sent a chill through her. "I was happy. And I'm going to San Francisco alone."

She rocked from side to side, rubbing Tyler's back. "We have to talk, Cash."

"Fine."

"When?"

"When I come back."

"When will that be?"

"I'm not sure. A few days. Maybe a week."

She looked at him for a long time, over the feathery newborn fuzz on their son's head. "All right, then," she said at last. "When you get back."

He returned in six days, flushed and happy, certain he'd made the deal of the century. He grabbed Abby around the waist and swung her in a circle—and her firm intention to sit down and talk with him just seemed to evaporate into the air.

Mrs. Helm served them a wonderful dinner, and afterward, they sat in the living room and talked. Tyler lay in Cash's lap, staring up at his father in what Abby would have sworn was pure adoration. Abby just couldn't bear to ruin such a lovely evening with a discussion of that awful agreement that she never, ever should have made.

Cash gave Tyler his bottle. Then, together, they put their son to bed.

After that, they went back to the living room for a
while. They listened to some music and talked some
more, about the computer chip deal, about how well Edna
was doing. And about Tess's new job at a gift shop over
on Main.

"She likes it," Abby said. "But I know she worries.
She doesn't make enough to save anything. And she's
bright. She wants more from life, for herself and for
Jobeth, you know?"

"Yeah. I know."

"She told me she got good grades in high school."

"So?"

"If someone helped her out a little, she could go to
college." Abby looked at her husband hopefully.

He shook his head. "Don't think I haven't tried. She
won't take that kind of help. She considers living with
Edna more charity than she should accept."

"But that's ridiculous. She's worked hard for Mom,
and she understands Mom. And Mom's been so hungry
for that, for another woman who puts value on what she
values. It's just meant everything to her."

Cash was grinning. "Some daughters would be jealous."

Abby shrugged. "What for? Just because I admire
Tess doesn't mean I want to be her. I like being me just
fine."

"I can understand why."

Abby met his eyes. She saw warmth and affection.
Admiration. And yes, love, too. And she was sure, at that
moment, that everything would work out all right.

She stood and stretched, thinking about the diaphragm
that Dr. Pruitt had prescribed for her. It waited in the
cabinet in the bathroom of the master suite, along with
the little tube of contraceptive jelly. Before she set about

seducing her husband, she had better put the darn thing where it would do some good.

"Tired?" Cash asked.

She smiled. "Not at all. But I think I'll just go get ready for bed."

"I have a few calls to make."

Something in his voice gave her pause. An edge? A wariness?

Best not to dwell on it. "That's fine," she said tenderly. She crossed the few feet between his chair and her chair and bent to kiss him, a light but lingering kiss. "Don't be too long," she said softly when she pulled away.

"I won't."

In the bathroom, she set to work putting the diaphragm in place. After a couple of false starts, she accomplished the task. That done, she rushed back into the bedroom, yanked off all of her clothes, wadded them up and tossed them in the corner of the closet. Then she slipped on a little scrap of black satin that she'd bought on her shopping trip to Billings the week before. Over it she wrapped a matching robe.

She went out into the main part of the bedroom to wait. First, she sat in a chair. Then she stretched out on the bed.

When Cash didn't appear after about twenty minutes, she went looking for him.

She found him in the study, on the phone. His eyes widened a little when he saw what she wore. She smiled invitingly and arched a questioning brow at him.

"Just a minute," he said into the mouthpiece. He punched the "mute" button. "Abby, I'm sorry. This is going to take a while."

She felt the smile fade from her lips. "How long?"

"I can't say. Just go on to bed, all right?"

She had that same urge she'd had last week when he'd called and said he wouldn't be home—the urge to scream and throw things. She quelled it, reminding herself how great the evening had been up until now.

"Okay," she replied carefully.

"Good night," he said, with way too much finality.

Abby returned to the master suite, where she traded her sexy outfit for a big T-shirt. In the bathroom, she removed the diaphragm, washed her face and cleaned her teeth. Then she crawled between the covers and turned off the light.

She laced her fingers behind her head and stared up at the dark ceiling and wondered where she'd gone wrong.

Maybe she hadn't been direct enough. She thought of their wedding night, some of her misery fading at the memory of how beautiful it had been. That night, she'd come right out and demanded that he make love with her. And he had given in to her demand—with a good deal of enthusiasm, in the end.

But on their wedding night, he'd been committed to trying to make their marriage work. Now she kept getting the feeling that he'd done all the "trying" he intended to do. And if she pushed him, he'd simply head out the door. Fast.

Abby sat up, lay back down, turned over. And admitted to herself that lovemaking—or the lack of it—was only a symptom of the real issue here.

The real issue was their marriage—which Abby felt more and more certain would not last.

At this rate, she feared, they'd never make it until July.

The dilemma remained the same: they had to talk about their problems. But she knew in her heart that as soon as they did, he would tell her that he wanted to be free.

Fearing she'd lose him, she put off confronting him. For weeks, they lived like polite acquaintances in the big house on North Street.

Cash wasn't around that much. The computer chip deal went bad, and he flew to San Francisco to try to salvage the situation. But it turned out that the chip just didn't live up to its advance PR. Cash lost a lot of money.

He could afford it. But it didn't make him happy. He wheeled and dealed all the harder to make back what he'd lost.

Abby took all the papers from the chip deal and went over them in depth. Then she made the mistake of announcing that he'd never have made that deal if she'd been there to advise him.

"Don't ride me, Abby," was all he said in response.

She had that urge to shout at him again. But she didn't. She held it in, somehow. And she went on holding it in, though more and more often, she wanted to scream at him.

Sometimes she saw desire in his eyes when he looked at her. But he never made a move on her. And she hated him for that. Because his unwillingness to make love with her could mean only one thing: he really did intend to leave her. Cash Bravo, after all, was much too noble a man to make love with his wife when he planned to divorce her.

Abby's anger grew. He had trapped her—oh, yes, he had. She loved him and she wanted him. But as soon as she really started fighting for him, she would lose him. She knew it as she knew that the sun set over the Big Horns.

And so she held her anger in.

Until a gray day in March, when some old pal of his called from Provo with a sob story about needing the down payment on a pickup truck.

Abby peeked in the doorway of Cash's study to tell him that Mrs. Helm had dinner on the table.

He was talking on the phone. "Tell you what, Earl," he said. "You name the figure, and I'll write the check."

Abby pushed the door open and leaned against the door frame, waiting for him to look her way.

Cash listened for a minute, then chuckled. "But, Earl, I don't need to see the truck. If you want it, you buy it. I'll wire you the down, and you pay me back when you can."

Earl said something else.

Cash made a low, amused sound in his throat. "Earl, Earl. I trust your judgment. You want it, you get it. And I'm glad to help you out.... Earl. Listen." Cash let out a long breath. "All right, all right. I'll fly on down there tonight." He chuckled again. "Well, Earl. I'm not Superman, you know?" He grabbed a pencil, scribbled something on a tablet. "You're in Provo, Earl. I'll need a few hours to get there." He scribbled some more, then ripped the page off the tablet and stuck it in a pocket. "I know, I know. But I tell you what. If somebody else snaps it up, we'll find you another one. I promise we will." He got up from his big calfskin swivel chair. "All right. Yeah. As soon as I can." He put the phone down, looked up—and saw Abby. "What?"

"Dinner," she said with great care, a numb kind of fury rising inside her. He was leaving again. Because some guy named Earl couldn't buy a pickup truck by himself.

Cash forked a hand back through his hair. "Look. Something's come up. I have to—"

"Take the Cessna to Provo to look at a pickup truck. I heard."

"Abby." His tone dripped reproach. "It's a favor. For an old friend."

She pasted on a smile over gritted teeth. "We'll come with you, Tyler and I."

"Don't be ridiculous. You can't drag the baby all the way to Provo just to look at a pickup truck."

"Watch me."

He tossed his pencil on the desk blotter. "All right. What's the problem?"

She glared at him. "I'm looking at it."

He made a faint groaning sound. "Oh. That's funny. Really funny."

"I don't think it's funny. Not at all." She stepped fully into the room and shut the door behind her, aware in every quivering nerve of her body that this was it. The big battle, the one she'd been avoiding by holding her temper. Well, her temper just wouldn't be held anymore. She could feel it straining at the leash of her good sense. It would break that leash. Very soon now.

He watched her close the door and then he sighed wearily. "Abby, let's not get into it. I have to go."

"No, you don't. You don't have to go. You can send Earl a nice, big check and he can either buy that pickup or not, his choice."

He shook his head. "You don't understand. It's not just about money. Earl's been going through a rough time lately and he could use a friend right now."

"Well, I can certainly understand that."

"Right," he muttered.

"I can, I swear. I'm kind of like Earl, really. Only could use a *husband* right now."

He came around the big desk. For a moment, she thought he would stride right up to her and confront her eye to eye. But he didn't. He wouldn't come that close. He kept several feet of gleaming hardwood floor between them.

"Abby, you know me. You've known me all your life. When a friend needs me, I help him. That's how I am."

She folded her arms under her breasts. "Great. Wonderful. Terrific. But what about your wife and son? What if we need you? Do we have to take a number and wait in line?"

He scowled at her, then he snorted. "You're being completely unreasonable. And I don't have time for it right now."

"You never have time. Not in weeks and weeks. And I am fed up."

He studied her. "You're fed up, huh?"

"Yes. I am."

"Well, all right, then. If you're fed up, you know what to do."

The words were cryptic. But she knew exactly what he meant by them. She dropped her arms, all the fight draining from her like water from a sieve.

"No, Cash," she said quietly. "I don't know what to do. That's the problem."

He looked away, then back. Like someone trapped. "Abby..."

"No. Please. Listen."

"Let's just not—"

"*Please.*"

He fell silent, though he didn't look happy about it.

She dragged in a breath and forged on. "I...I want to

reach out to you, but you won't let me. I want to get close to you again, but you're so far away. Help me, Cash. Tell me. What can I do to work things out with you?"

He looked at her for the longest time. And then he turned away. He stuck his hands in his pockets and stared at a couple of Remington prints on the far wall.

"Cash."

"Yeah?" He still didn't look at her.

She swallowed. "Cash, please...." She took a step toward him.

He turned back to her then and put up a hand. "Look. Just don't, okay?"

"But it's all...falling apart. We hardly see each other. We never...make love...."

He winced. "Stop."

But she wouldn't stop. "We had so much last summer and in Boulder. We got along so well. We were happy. At least, I know *I* was happy. Were you?"

"Abby—"

"Just tell me. Were you happy?"

He lifted one shoulder in sort of a half shrug. "Yeah. All right. I was happy."

"So what happened?"

He went on looking at her, but he didn't answer her question.

She felt as if they stood on opposite sides of the world. Somehow, she had to bridge the distance. Though his eyes warned her to keep back, she took a step toward him. And then another.

When she stood only inches from him, she whispered, "Cash. Please. You said we would talk about this, about *us*, after the baby came. Well, the baby's here. The baby's been here for months. And you just won't talk."

"I don't think..." His voice faded off.

"What? You don't think what?"

He closed his eyes, tipped his head toward the ceiling. "That there's much to say."

Her anger sparked again. "What do you mean, there's not much to say? You're my husband. I'm your wife. I want to spend the rest of my life with you."

He looked right at her, and didn't say a word. "Hell."

She threw up her hands. "What? What does that look mean? Talk to me, Cash. I've had enough of you sighing and shaking your head and turning away."

"You won't like it if I talk to you."

"Do it anyway."

"Fine." He sank to the edge of the desk, his big shoulders slumping. "Abby, I...this isn't working out. I'm not cut out for marriage. You knew it from the first. We gave it a good try, but—"

Though she'd demanded that he talk to her, now she couldn't bear to let him finish. She cut in, "No, we didn't. We didn't give it nearly enough of a try. If you'll only listen to me, you'll understand that we need to—"

"Abby, I'm through."

"No. That's not true. Don't say that. I won't accept that."

"You have to accept it."

"No—"

"Abby, it takes two to make a marriage. And I want out. You asked me, I'm telling you. I want that divorce. There's no point in waiting until July. You get yourself a decent lawyer. And we'll get it over with."

"But I don't want it over with. I just want *you*."

"Abby..."

"No. Wait." She couldn't stand it. She'd known this was coming. But now that it was here, she only wanted to stop, to go back to the moment before she'd pushed him to talk to her. "Listen. Let's just forget this. Let's just go on as if I hadn't said anything."

He looked at her with such sadness. And pity.

Shameless now, she couldn't stop begging. "Please. Listen. Cash, we can make it work. Just give it a chance. You know that we can!"

He stood from the edge of the desk. "Abby..."

She threw herself against him, grabbing his shirt in her fists. "Listen. Please. I want to make it work. We have to make it work." I love you, she thought. But she couldn't quite say it. It had always been too dangerous to say it. Only once had she dared, on the night when she thought she would die.

And a lot of good it had done her.

"Cash..."

"No."

"Don't tell me no!"

"Abby, it's over."

She wouldn't hear it. She *refused* to hear it. With a low, desperate cry, she surged up—and captured his mouth before he could say any more.

He froze. And then he moaned.

She moaned back, in triumph and in hope. Because she could feel it—the shock of connection. The yearning. The hunger between them.

She pressed herself against him, her hands sliding up to wrap around his neck. And he responded, his mouth devouring hers, his arms like bands of steel around her, his hands roaming her back.

And then he stiffened. He tore his mouth away.

She clutched him tighter. "No, please. Please, Cash..."

But it didn't help. He took her arms and peeled them

away. He looked down at her, his eyes like blue chips of ice.

"Stop. Just stop."

She stared at him for the longest time, into those cold, stranger's eyes. And then, very calmly, she commanded, "Let go of me."

He released her. She stepped back, turned away, tried to collect her shattered wits.

But all she could think of were the days and days she'd waited and hoped. And for nothing. To have it end like this. Over some old buddy of his and a pickup.

With him looking so distant and cold. And with her begging him.

Had all those other women begged him?

If they had, she was just like them now. And if they hadn't, she was less than them. Because she hadn't even managed to salvage her pride.

Now he was the one approaching her. He came up behind her, gently grasped her shoulders. She shrugged off his touch.

"Abby," he said.

His kindly tone set her teeth on edge.

"Once you get used to it, you'll see that it's for the best. You'll have your freedom and I'll have mine. And Tyler will get both of us, just the way we always planned it."

The way *you* planned it, she thought, though she didn't say it out loud.

He went on, "You'll always have whatever you want."

Except what I want most: you.

"I'll instruct my lawyer to give you anything you ask for."

It was too much. She whirled on him. "Forget it. If

you won't be my husband, I don't need or want anything from you. I can take care of myself just fine.''

"I'll always take care of you."

"No, you won't. Because I won't let you."

"Abby, you're acting like a child."

"Right. Call me a child. That's always your defense against me. I'm a child, and so you don't have to take me seriously. You don't have to listen to me. You don't have to love me like the woman you know I really am!"

"Abby, settle down."

She backed away from him, because if she didn't, she would have jumped on him—and not to kiss him this time. "Get this. I don't care about your money. I don't *want* your money."

"Come on, don't be like this."

"I won't take a damn penny from you, Cash Bravo. You won't ease your conscience about me by buying me off." She backed into the credenza against the wall by the door.

"Abby, stop it." He took a careful step toward her. "This is for the best. You'll see that I'm right as soon as you cool down a little and start to think rationally."

"Rationally? *Rationally?*" She felt behind her, and her fingers closed around the base of something heavy. She picked it up and brought it around so she could see it: a bronze figurine of a cowboy on a rearing horse.

"Abby, put that thing down."

Nothing in the world would have given her greater pleasure than to smash him in the face with it.

"Abby, come on...."

She settled for waving it at him, feeling like a fool, hating him almost as much as she loved him. "Out!" She felt the tears rising. She couldn't stand for him to see them. "Get out of this house."

"Abby—"

"Just get out. Pack a bag and go to Provo."

He closed his eyes. Drew in a deep breath. "All right. Fine." He strode to the door, pulled it open.

"Don't come back," she said.

He went out the door, closing it quietly behind him. She waited, holding her breath, until she was certain he was really gone. Then, carefully, she set down the bronze statue.

She gulped and swallowed, making ludicrous choking sounds, trying to hold the blasted tears back. But they wouldn't be held.

They spilled down her face. Gulping, sobbing, despising herself for giving in to such weakness, she went to the big desk and dropped into the calfskin swivel chair. She put her arms on the blotter and laid her head down and let the tears have their way.

Fifteen minutes later, she raised her head and slumped back in the chair. She shuddered. An animal cry tried to get out. She forced it down. With the back of her hand, she wiped her nose. She put both palms flat on the blotter and pushed herself to her feet.

Not far away, on the side table by a leather love seat, sat a box of tissues. Abby marched over there, grabbed a handful and blew her nose repeatedly. Then she squared her shoulders, smoothed her hair and went out to sit down to dinner alone.

Chapter Fifteen

For the next two days, Abby didn't leave the house. She took care of her baby and ate when Mrs. Helm put the food on the table. She went through the motions of living. And she did not cry again.

The third day was Saturday, one of Mrs. Helm's two days off. There was no breakfast on the table. So after giving Tyler his early bottle, Abby went back to bed. She pulled the covers close around her, shut her eyes and dropped into a fitful, unsatisfying sleep.

The phone rang at nine. She groped on the night stand and found it. "What?"

"Well. Good morning to you, too."

"Mom."

"You sound so *happy* to hear from me."

"I was sleeping."

"Then it's time you got up. I'm coming by."

"No!"

A silence, then, "All right. What's wrong?"

She didn't want to think about it. She only wanted to go back to sleep.

"Abigail."

But could she afford to go back to sleep, really?

"Abigail, I don't like this."

No. She couldn't.

Fact: her husband had left her. The marriage that was supposed to have lasted at least a year had barely survived for nine months in the end.

She had told him she wouldn't take his money, yet here she lay in his bed, her stomach rumbling because his housekeeper hadn't come in today to feed her.

She needed a job, not more sleep.

"Abigail, I'm coming over there."

She shoved back the covers. "Don't bother. Tyler and I will be over at your place in half an hour. There's something we have talk about."

"I don't like the sound of this."

"You think you don't like it now, wait until I get there."

"Abigail, Abigail," Edna murmured sadly as she stood at the stove, poaching eggs. "Didn't I warn you that this would happen? You should have taken better care of that man."

Abby, at the table, shifted her son to her other arm. "I did take good care of Cash."

Edna took the lid from the pan, lifted the poaching tray out of the water and turned the two eggs into a cup. "I'm sure you believe you did."

Abby pulled in a deep breath and assumed a peacemaking tone. "Let's not argue about it, Mom. I did the best I could. And I suppose you're right—it wasn't good enough.''

Edna carried the eggs to her daughter, along with a plate of golden brown toast. "Here. Eat. Give me that beautiful boy." Abby handed Tyler to his grandmother and picked up her spoon. Holding Tyler on one arm, Edna got the coffeepot with her free hand and refilled the two cups on the table. Then she sat and watched her daughter eat.

Abby looked up from the meal. "Thanks, Mom. These eggs are perfect."

"You need your strength."

"Amen."

Gently, Edna rocked Tyler. "He looks just like his daddy."

"Do I need to hear that right now?"

Edna glanced up from the baby. "It's not something you'll ever escape. Face it. You'll think of that man all your life. Every time you look at this boy." She leaned toward Abby a little and lowered her voice. "You love him. And you have to find a way to get him back."

Abby thought of his cold eyes, of the way she had begged him. "I don't want him back."

Edna retreated to her own chair. "That's only pride talking."

"So? What's wrong with a woman having a little pride?"

"It won't keep you warm in a blizzard."

"It's better than nothing."

"Not by much." She looked sideways at Abby. "I don't know how you can let him go. He loves you so. I'll bet his heart is broken."

"Mom. Try to get it straight. *He* left *me*."

"What does that matter? I know he didn't *want* to leave you."

"Oh. And just how do you know that?"

"A million ways. The way he looks when you come in the room. The way he lights up when he hears your voice or when I talk about you. I know Cash. After all, I as good as raised him from the time he was ten years old. And I've been watching him since the two of you married. He loves you."

Abby sipped some coffee, then set the cup down firmly. "Sure he loves me. And he loves you. He loves Nate and Zach and Tess and Jobeth. And some guy named Earl in Provo."

"You know what I mean. He loves you as a man loves a woman. He loves you deeply. He loves you more than he's ever loved any other person on this earth."

"He has a strange way of showing it."

"You could get him back if you tried."

"Look. I don't want to talk about it anymore."

"Fine, fine. Ruin your life."

"Mom. I didn't come here to argue."

"No, you came here to listen to some good advice."

"I did not."

"Oh? Then what?"

"I need your help."

Edna frowned. "What kind of help?"

"I want to get a job."

"A job?" Edna rolled her eyes. "You don't need a job. Even if you've driven him away, Cash will always take care of you. That's the way he is."

Silently, Abby reminded herself that she wanted her mother's help—and if she started yelling at her, she probably wouldn't get it. With great patience, she explained for what seemed like the hundredth time, "I don't want him taking care of me. I want to take care of myself."

"Oh, I do not understand you. I will never understand you."

"Will you help me, Mom?"

Edna released a long, weary breath. "What kind of job?"

"I don't really know yet. But I have the better part of a business degree. So I think I can find something. But I need you to look after Tyler for me while I look. And then, when I do find something, I would want you to watch him while I'm working."

"This baby needs his mother."

"And this mother needs a job. Will you help me or not?"

Edna smoothed the blanket around Tyler's sleeping face. "What a little angel. A beautiful, perfect angel."

"Mother. Will you help me?"

"Just like his daddy."

"Mother. Yes or no?"

"Oh, do what you have to do. And I'll take care of this beautiful boy whenever you need me to."

"Thanks."

"But I won't stop hoping that you and Cash will work things out."

Abby pushed the remains of her toast away. "He's left me, Mother. And I don't want him back. Get used to it, because that's the way it is." She looked over and saw that Tess was standing in the arch that led to the living room. "Come on in. The coffee's hot."

"I don't believe what I just heard," Tess said. "Cash would never leave you."

"Believe it," Abby replied. "And can we please talk about something else?"

Just then the door to the garage flew open. Jobeth stood on the concrete steps beyond the threshold, soaking wet and shivering. "Mom!" she wailed.

"What happened?" Edna demanded as Tess hurried over and ushered her daughter into the warmth of the room.

Jobeth began babbling something about the boy down the street, a gate and a bucket of water rigged to a string in a cottonwood tree.

"You got doused," Tess said.

"I am never playing with that Nick Collerby again," Jobeth whined.

"Come on," Tess said. "Dry clothes. Now."

"Why would he do that to me, Mom?"

"I haven't the faintest idea. We'll get you dry, and you can go ask him."

"I will not ask him. I *can't* ask him. I'm not speaking to him. Ever again for as long as I live...."

Patiently, Tess herded her toward the stairs.

Edna grinned at Abby. "Children. Always up to something."

Abby stared at her mother, wishing she'd been one tenth that serene while Abby was growing up.

Moments later, Tess and Jobeth reappeared and Tess got to work making hot chocolate for Jobeth.

"Use the double boiler," Edna instructed. "It's down in that cabinet there."

Tess bent down and looked in the cabinet. "I don't see it, Edna."

Clucking her tongue, Edna handed Tyler to Abby and went to find the pans herself.

Abby cradled her son, enjoying the warmth of the kitchen and the chatter of the others. She also felt relief that her mother had agreed to look after Tyler—and that the subject of herself and Cash seemed to be closed.

Tess appeared at Abby's door at eight that night.

Abby looked at the other woman with suspicion. "Is this about Cash?"

Tess shivered. "It's really cold out here, Abby."

"All right, all right." Abby stepped back and let Tess into the house.

In the living room, Tess perched on the edge of the sofa. "I just, well, I can't stop thinking about what I heard today. It makes no sense at all. You and Cash love each other. And you were meant to be together."

Abby sat in the caramel-colored leather chair and fiddled with the little carved box in which Cash kept the cigarettes he was always trying not to smoke.

"Abby. Talk to me."

Abby shut the lid of the box with a snap. "Look. He doesn't want to be married. He is not a marrying kind of man. He only married me because of Tyler, because we didn't...take precautions. And I got pregnant."

"It happens that way sometimes."

Something in Tess's voice tipped Abby off. The women shared a long glance. Finally, Abby asked, "You and Josh?"

Tess nodded. She looked down at her hands, which were folded in her lap. "I was seventeen." She raised her head, gave Abby a sad smile. "And he was so handsome. We had nothing in common. It was just one of those things that happen, between a foolish girl...and a reckless man.

"When I found out I was pregnant, he said he'd marry me. It seemed like the best choice at the time. But we were so different. He couldn't stay in one place—and all

I wanted was to go home.'' She relaxed back onto the couch, her eyes far away now, lost somewhere in the past. ''My parents had a ranch. In South Dakota. I always thought that in the end I'd go back there. But my mother lost it after my father died. And I can't ever go back.''

''I'm so sorry....''

Tess shook her head. ''Don't be. I do have Jobeth. She's a big consolation for...everything that might have been.''

Abby thought of the baby sleeping in the other room. ''I know exactly what you mean.''

''No, you don't.''

Abby blinked. ''What?''

''You don't know what I mean. You can't know. You and Cash aren't anything like me and Josh. You and Cash are a good match.''

''Tess...''

''You are. Better than good. You're exactly right for each other. I knew it the first time I saw you together.''

Abby made a disbelieving sound. ''Tell that to Cash.''

''I would. If he was here.''

''Well, he's not. Because he doesn't want me.''

''Oh, come on.''

''He doesn't.''

''Of course he does. I was there, remember, the night Tyler was born? I saw with my own eyes how Cash feels about you. He loves you more than his life. You just have to find out why he thinks it's best for you if he leaves you. Because believe me, that's the only reason he would do what he's done.''

Abby stared at Tess. ''You think that Cash has walked out on me...for my own good?''

''I *know* that's what he's done.''

Right then, looking at Tess's earnest face, Abby found

herself wanting to believe—and thinking of how she had once imagined that Tess was in love with Cash. She had a crazy urge right then to ask her friend if there might be any truth to her suspicion. But to ask would be to cross some invisible boundary. And Abby didn't know if she could deal with what she'd find on the other side.

"When you love someone, *really* love someone," Tess said softly, "you want what's best for them, no matter what the cost to yourself."

A tight laugh escaped Abby. "But he won't talk to me. I've reasoned with him, I've yelled at him. I've tried everything. You just don't know...."

Tess smiled her gentle smile. "Have you actually told him that you love him?"

Abby looked away, then made herself meet her friend's eyes again. "Once."

"And?"

"It didn't do any good. If anything, I think it pushed him away. Like I said, he's not a marrying man. Talk of love makes him really nervous."

Tess stood. "So he needs to get adjusted to hearing it. You have to tell him again. You have to tell him a *lot.*"

"But Tess, he won't *let* me tell him. Every time I try, he puts me off or walks away—or says he wants a divorce."

Tess moved around the coffee table and came to stand before Abby's chair. "Then you must be relentless."

"I've been relentless."

"Not relentless enough."

"I'm just..." Abby hung her head.

"What?"

Abby let out a long sigh. "So tired. Of having him reject me."

Tess dropped to her knees in front of Abby. "Of

course you are. But tell the truth. Do you want to spend the rest of your life without him?''

''Oh, Tess...''

''Well?''

''No!'' It was a cry of longing. ''I want him back. I want him beside me.''

''Then go after him.''

''He won't give me the chance.''

''Make the chance. And don't let your foolish pride get in the way this time.''

Abby hardly slept all night. She tossed and turned, thinking of the things that Tess had said. By the time the first rays of the sun were turning the sky orange-yellow in the east, she had decided to give winning Cash Bravo one more try.

She talked to her son as she fed him and dressed him, explaining that he would have to stay with his grandma for a few days, but when she returned, she would bring his daddy back with her. ''And from then on, Tyler, I swear to you. We will take you with us, wherever we go.''

She prayed she wasn't lying. To her son. Or to herself.

Once she had Tyler ready, she searched Cash's office, checking for an address that might belong to Earl, in Provo, last name unknown. She came up with zero; she'd have to look elsewhere.

''I might be gone a few days, Mom,'' she said when she showed up at Edna's to drop off Tyler.

Edna let out a small cry of dismay. ''You're looking for a job out of town?''

''I'm not looking for a job.''

''Then what?''

"I just don't want to go into it now. Please understand."

And it seemed as if she actually did. At least she stopped asking questions.

She kissed Abby's cheek. "You call me. Let me know where you are."

Abby promised that she would.

And then she headed over to Main Street, and Cash's storefront office there. Abby let herself in with the key that Cash had given her years ago, during the first summer she came to work for him.

Inside, Renata's cluttered desk sat in the center of the rectangular room, with two chairs for visitors facing it. Renata wasn't in yet, of course. She rarely showed up before eleven and it was just past eight.

Abby headed straight for the desk. She booted up the computer and ran a search on the name "Earl" in the word processor address book she had taught Renata to use. No luck. Either Earl had never actually dealt with Cash Ventures, or Renata wasn't keeping up the file.

Abby tried the Rolodex, thumbing through every card since she didn't have a last name. Either she missed it, or Earl wasn't there.

With a sigh, she picked up the phone and called Renata at home. Cash's secretary answered on the fourth ring.

"Huh?"

"Hi, Renata. It's me," Abby said cheerily. "I'm really sorry to wake you, but I've got a question for you."

"Uh. Yeah. Huh?"

"Do you recall a guy Cash knows named Earl, in Provo?"

"Uh. Earl. Sure."

"I can't remember his last name. Can you?"

"Uh." Renata yawned and sighed. "He just goes by Earl, I think."

"I was afraid of that. What's his address?"

"Uh."

There was a long pause. Abby feared Renata might have grown suspicious—or gone back to sleep. But she was only thinking.

"Oh, yeah," she said at last. "I remember. Cash called on Thursday. He gave me Earl's address and phone number just in case."

"Great. Where is it?"

"It's, um...the Rolodex?"

"I looked there. Didn't find it."

"Well, I *meant* to put it in the Rolodex...."

"Fine, Renata." Abby assumed her best fed-up employer voice. "But it's not there."

"Well, I don't...oh. Wait. Look under my coffee cup. There's a notepad."

Abby lifted Renata's coffee cup, which was shaped like a smiling cat with a tail for a handle. Underneath she found the notepad—and on it, Earl's address and phone number, only partly obscured by a dried coffee ring. "Here it is."

"Good."

"Go back to sleep."

"I will. Oh. Ab?"

"What?"

"Did you want Cash—is that it?"

Abby felt her stomach knot up. "Why?"

"Because he left Earl's on Friday."

Abby muttered something rude as she dropped into the chair behind the desk. All this silly sneaking around when she could have just come right out and asked.

"Did you try that cell phone of his?" Renata asked.

Abby hadn't. She considered the phone a last resort. She wanted to track him down and confront him face to face.

"Where is he now?" Abby asked.

"The Nugget in Reno. I scribbled his room number somewhere...oh, yeah, I remember. The lower right-hand corner of the desk blotter. See it?"

"Well..." The blotter was a virtual explosion of scribbles and doodles.

"It's in purple ink, under a green smiley face, with a—"

"Right. I got it." She grabbed one of the hundred or so scraps of paper stuck under the edges of the blotter and wrote the number down. "What's he there for? A card game?"

"No, some meetings with Redbone Deevers and some investor group, about a time-share condo deal, I think." Renata paused to yawn again hugely. "He'll be there until Tuesday, he said."

Abby went back to the house to pack a small bag and line up a flight. Then she drove to Sheridan, to the small airport there.

She didn't touch down in Reno until late afternoon. She took a cab to the Nugget, which was actually in nearby Sparks. At the Nugget, she went straight up to the room whose number Renata had provided on the chance that Cash might be there, between meetings on the condo deal. She set her suitcase on the carpet, took three deep breaths and then knocked.

After what seemed like forever, she heard the lock turn on the other side. The door swung open. And Abby found herself face to face with a beautiful blonde in a slinky pink silk robe. "Yes?" the blonde asked politely.

Abby saw red. "All right. Where is he?"

"What? Excuse me?"

"Who is it, darling?" A man Abby had never seen before appeared in the door to the bedroom behind the blonde.

Abby gulped. "Er, I'm looking for my husband. Cash Bravo?"

The blonde and the strange man exchanged glances. "Sorry," the woman said. "No one by that name here." Swiftly and firmly, she shut the door in Abby's face.

Abby stared at the door for a moment, feeling foolish and lost. Then she picked up her suitcase and went down to the main desk.

The clerk punched some buttons on the keyboard of his reservations computer, then he shook his head. "I'm sorry. Mr. Bravo checked out this morning."

The desk clerk said he'd watch her suitcase, so she left it with him while she found a phone and called Renata. But Renata hadn't heard from Cash, not since he'd called to tell her he'd be staying at the Nugget. She gave in and tried Cash's cell phone: no answer.

She was just hanging up in despair, when a voice several feet away drawled, "I'll be damned. Is that you, kid?"

She turned to find Redbone Deevers lumbering toward her on his ebony cane. She ran to him and he enfolded her in a bear hug. Then he stepped back. She looked up into his broad face with its fringe of white hair. He sported a goatee and favored white three-piece suits. To Abby, he always seemed the image of the courtly Southern gentleman, though Cash claimed he'd been born in Detroit, son of a steel-mill worker and a grocery-store clerk.

"Investors like a little glamour and romance," Cash

had told Abby. "So Redbone gives them what they want."

Now Redbone was looking appropriately concerned and solemn. "You come after that husband of yours?"

She nodded.

"Well, he's gone."

"I know. They told me at the desk."

"We finished our business. And profitably, too." His white eyebrows lifted. "You come to work things out with him?"

"Oh, Redbone..."

He patted her shoulder with his big, gentle hand. "Now, now. Come on over here. Sit yourself down." He led her to a pair of black leather chairs against a nearby wall.

Once they were both settled, she dared to demand, "All right, what did Cash tell you?"

"Not a thing." Redbone shrugged. "But you weren't with him. And he growled at me like a flea-bit hound when I asked him how you were doin'. I drew my own conclusions."

"I see."

He leaned a little closer. "You want to know where he's gone?"

Hope made her sit up a little straighter. "You know?"

Redbone chuckled. "He said he had a yen to get away from it all. Can you believe that? Cash Bravo with a yen to get away from it all?"

"It doesn't sound much like him."

"No, it does not. But I couldn't stand to see him looking so glum. So I offered him the use of my private cabin on the lake."

"Did he take it?"

"He did."

"Where is it?"

The old gentleman looked at her sideways. "Is he goin' to be unhappy with old Redbone when you show up lookin' for him?"

Right then, someone hit a jackpot on a slot machine not twenty yards away. Bells clanged and lights flashed. Abby glanced over to where the winner stood calmly, watching the river of coins as it poured into the tray.

"You ever heard the old story about how Cash got his name?"

She looked at Redbone. "I've heard it."

"One too many times, I'll bet."

Abby shrugged. She was more interested in finding her husband than in discussing what an amusing child he had been.

Redbone asked, with a gleam in his eye, "You goin' to answer my question?"

She confessed, "The truth is, he'll probably be mad at you if you tell me where he's gone."

Redbone laughed, a deep, belly-shaking sound. "Well, that's just fine. Let 'im steam. I can take it."

She leaned toward Redbone again. "Tell me, then."

"Fair enough. Got a pen?"

It was a sixty-mile trip from the Reno-Sparks area to Redbone's hideaway in the pines on the shore of Lake Tahoe. Abby took a cab. Darkness had fallen by the time the cab pulled into the clear space in front of the cabin.

Abby, in the back seat, looked out the side window at the tall, shadowy trees. In the distance, far across the black water, she could see snow-tipped mountains, as rough and craggy as the mountains of home. A sliver of moon hung over the highest peak, a bright star above it, so it seemed as if the moon swung from that star.

"This is it, lady," the cabdriver said. "And it looks to me like nobody's home."

Abby stared out the other window, toward the dark cabin, which appeared shut up tight. There was no sign of another vehicle anywhere, either.

"Could you wait here for a minute?"

"No problem."

Abby got out of the car and pulled her coat close around her against the night chill. She mounted the rustic steps and pounded on the heavy door. And then she waited.

No lights came on. And there was no sound from inside.

She went down the steps and around to the back, which turned out to be just as dark and deserted as the front of the place. With the key Redbone had given her, she let herself in the back door.

The cabin was as rustic inside as out, with unfinished furniture and a set of deer antlers over the potbellied stove in the main room. It didn't take long to look through the whole place. And to find that there was no one there.

"Where to now, lady?" the cabbie asked wearily when Abby climbed into the back seat once more.

"Back to the Nugget," she said.

When she trudged into the Nugget again, Abby went straight to the front desk and asked for a room.

Once she'd checked in, she tried Cash's cell phone again and again and got no answer. Once she'd hung up, she considered calling her mother. But she felt too depressed to pick up the phone another time. And besides, she'd be talking to Edna soon enough. Because she would be on the first flight she could get tomorrow, headed for home.

It had been a crazy idea anyway to go chasing after Cash. Clearly, he didn't want to be found.

The trip home took forever. As on the flight to Reno, she had to go to Denver and then board a puddle jumper for Sheridan. The sun had long ago disappeared behind the Big Horns when she finally got off the highway in Medicine Creek.

She drove straight to her mother's. "Mom, I just want my baby," she said when Edna opened the door.

"Then go on home," Edna replied. "Your baby's there. With your husband, where he belongs."

Chapter Sixteen

Abby dropped her coat, purse and suitcase inside the front door and went looking for her husband and her son. She found them in the baby's room. Cash was sitting in the rocker, feeding Tyler his bottle.

He looked up and saw her standing in the doorway. He whispered roughly, "Where've you been?"

She felt so many emotions her body could hardly contain them all. Joy. Rage. Hurt. Relief. Hopeless, incurable love most of all, flooding through her, warming her flesh and weakening her knees. She swallowed and replied in a whisper as rough as his had been, "Looking for you."

He scanned her face. Then he glanced down at the child in his arms. "He's almost done."

She leaned in the doorway, waiting. Tyler finished his meal. Cash set the bottle aside and carefully lifted the small body to his broad shoulder. He rose from the rocker and came to stand before her. "Here." Gently, he held out their son.

She took his small, warm weight in her arms, brought him close to her heart. She snuggled his wobbly head beneath her chin and he burped against her neck.

Cash whispered, "He's ready to go down."

She looked into her husband's face—and felt anger rising. Without a word, she turned from him and went to sit in the rocker.

Cash stayed in the doorway. She could feel him there, watching her. But she didn't look at him. She closed her eyes and rocked her baby. And when she opened her eyes again, Cash had gone.

Tyler needed changing, so she performed the task. His sleepy eyes kept drooping as she cleaned him up. Once the job was done, she laid him in his bed and kissed the back of his warm little head. Already off in dreamland somewhere, he made no sound when she turned off the light.

She found Cash in their bedroom, sitting in one of the two big chairs beneath the window that faced the side yard. He looked at her when she appeared from the short hall off the living room, but he didn't say anything. Feeling nervous and wary—and more angry as each moment passed—Abby entered the room. She went straight to the bed, dropped to the end of it and kicked off her shoes.

She could feel Cash's eyes on her, though he remained silent. Leaning defiantly back on her hands, she looked at him. "Well?"

Still he said nothing, only shifted in the chair.

She waited, daring him to speak.

Finally, he did. "I'm scared to death."

She knew that—had known it all along, deep in her

heart. And she had ached for him, that love frightened him so. But right then, she was dealing with her own pain—pain he had caused her. And she just couldn't drum up much sympathy for him.

"You're still mad at me, aren't you?"

She let several grim seconds go by before answering, "Furious."

He shifted in the chair again, but he still looked far from comfortable.

And that was just fine with her. She didn't want him comfortable.

"Abby, come on. Talk to me. Please."

She let out a low, rageful sound and sat up straight. "I begged you," she said, the words tight, brimming with her fury and love and pain. "*Begged* you."

"Abby..."

All at once, she couldn't just sit there. She jumped to her feet and turned on him, clenching her hands at her sides to keep them from reaching out and closing around his neck. "I am not someone who begs."

"I know."

Slowly and deliberately, she said the words: "I love you."

He had the grace not to wince or turn away. "I know."

She held her head high and she told him with pride, "I have always loved you."

"Abby, I—"

"No. Let me say it."

"But I—"

"I want you to just sit there and listen to me. *Really* listen. For once."

His blue gaze moved over her face, heartbreakingly intent. "All right."

She needed to move. So she paced the floor, back and

forth from the bureau to the bed. Finally, she had her thoughts in order. She stopped, turned to face him.

"Since I was a little girl, I've loved you. Do you know that?"

He closed his eyes, breathed deeply—and nodded.

She went on, "But I knew so much about you, knew you were afraid of loving. So I tried, for years and years, to pretend that the love I felt for you was an innocent love. But it wasn't."

She paused, daring him to interrupt. He didn't, so she made herself continue. "Finally, the time came when I couldn't pretend anymore. I..." She swallowed convulsively. "I reached for you. As a woman, I reached for you...the night they buried my dad. And you reached for me. As a man."

Suddenly she couldn't look into those knowing blue eyes for one second longer. She turned, spoke to the far wall. "We...made Tyler. And we married. But still, you held back." She whirled to face him again, forced herself to confess, "Oh, I did, too, I know. I held back, too. I suggested that stupid agreement. I told you I wanted a temporary marriage, instead of admitting from the first that, as far as I was concerned, there was never anything temporary about you and me. I was afraid to say my love out loud. And I never did. For all those years I was growing up—and right into our married life together. I never, ever said my love out loud. Because I knew I would lose you if I did."

She looked toward the dark window behind his head. "And I was right. When I tried to get you to throw out the agreement, you wouldn't. You told me to wait. Until the baby came. Until I was—" she paused, then sneered "—more myself." She grimaced at him. "That was how you put it, wasn't it?"

His lips thinned; he coughed. Then he muttered, "Yes."

She went on, "And then the baby did come. And it all happened just the way I always knew it would. The night Tyler was born, I did it. I said my love out loud. And from that night, you started to leave me." She stared right at him, hard and long. "That is what happened, isn't it?"

He nodded.

"And in the end, when you said you were going, I threw out the one thing I had always kept for myself when it came to you—my pride. I *begged* you to stay. But you wouldn't." A chill shook her body. She wrapped her arms around her middle. "And that was it, the final straw. I told myself I wouldn't take any more. That I was through with you.

"But then my mother started in on me. And Tess, too. Both of them telling me how you loved me. I could brush my mother off. But not Tess. She was so...convincing. She insisted that you would never leave me unless you thought it was best for me. And that, well, it kind of made sense."

She shivered some more, hugged herself harder. "So I chased you. All the way to Reno and Lake Tahoe, I chased you. But I couldn't find you."

"Because I came home."

She stared at him, loving him so, almost wishing she didn't.

He must have known he had some explaining to do.

Grimly, he admitted, "Tess was right, up to a point."

"How?"

"I told myself that I was doing the best thing for you."

"To leave me?"

"Yes. I told myself it was the right thing to do, to use that stupid agreement we'd made to set you free."

"The *right* thing?"

"Yeah. Because you're so young. You have so much ahead of you. And I...I took the choices away from you. I made love to you and got you pregnant. And I pushed you to go back to school. It was all too much for you. Because of the choices I made, you nearly died."

She felt totally exhausted, suddenly. She dropped to the edge of the bed once more. "Oh, Cash, when will you give me credit for being part of those choices, too?"

"I will. I do now. Just let me finish."

She cast him a glance, then looked down at the floor. "Okay. Fine. Finish."

"I know you were there, too. That *we* made those choices. But I wouldn't admit it to myself or to you. I was too busy being noble, the way you always said. Out saving the damn world. Saving you. From me. So I wouldn't have to deal with how scared I am...to love you."

Abby closed her eyes. He had said it. He had as good as said it. She asked in a voice that was torn at the edges, "And *do* you, then? Do you love me?"

"More than I've loved anything or anyone ever. I swear to you."

Those words meant so much. Abby felt her hurt and anger fading, melting away like snow in the path of a chinook.

They stood at the same time.

"You were right," he said. "I was happy when I was a little kid. And I've hated my father for turning away from me when he lost my mother. I didn't want to get hurt that way again. But when you almost died, I saw it happening to me. Just as it happened to me when I was a kid. Just like it happened to my father, losing the one who mattered most. And I thought...I could escape it. By turning away from you. But I didn't escape it. I only...lost you." He made a low, anguished sound. "You *hadn't* died, after all. And still I'd lost you...."

"Oh, Cash..."

"And I was setting myself up to lose Tyler, too. Doing the same thing my father did to me. Turning away, cutting him out. I don't want to be like that. Help me, Abby. Help me not to be like that...." He took a step toward her.

She took one toward him.

He held out his arms.

And then she was flying—straight to where she wanted to be. He crushed her close, his whole body trembling. She held on tight.

He let out a long, shuddering breath. And then he took her by the shoulders and looked into her eyes. "I love you, Abby. You can't know how much."

She wondered if it could be legal to feel happiness like this.

"Abby, we never should have made that crazy agreement."

"I know."

"I want to throw it out. I want you to be my wife. For real. Forever. Will you do that? Will you stay with me?"

She reached up, laid her hand on his cheek. "It seems I've waited my whole life for you to ask me that."

"Are you saying you will?"

She pulled his head down so his mouth hovered just above hers, on the brink of a kiss. "Oh, Cash. Yes. I will."

He whispered her name as his lips met hers.

Epilogue

Meggie May Kane stood at the edge of the dance floor that had been set up under the stars for the Fourth of July dance. It was just like old times, she thought, with the lanterns strung overhead, the bandstand, the dance floor—and the red, white and blue bunting looped everywhere. When Meggie was growing up, the Community Club used to put on a dance every Fourth. But lately, the custom had been lost. Then, this year, the Medicine Creek Merchant's Society had decided to revive the tradition. They'd done a beautiful job of it.

The band struck up a slow number. The lines of dancers broke, milled and re-formed into pairs. Embracing couples swayed and turned across the floor. Meggie watched Cash and Abby Bravo. They'd been married about a year now. And they looked so happy it almost hurt to watch them.

Once, Meggie had dreamed of happiness like that....

Swallowing down pointless tears, Meggie turned from the dance floor. There were a few rows of chairs set up in front of the bandstand. Meggie sank into one of them. As the music played, neighbors and family friends approached her.

"Meggie, I'm so sorry about your dad."

"How are you doin' there, Meggie?"

"Meggie, we're thinking of you. Our hearts go out..."

Meggie murmured her thanks for their kind words and tried not to show her pain and fury. Her father's funeral had taken place just the day before. She had loved him so much. And yet right now, she was so angry with him she couldn't even think of him without wanting to throw back her head and scream in rage.

But what good would that do? Jason Kane was far beyond anybody's wrath now.

"Meggie?"

She looked up—and smiled when she saw who it was. "Zach. How are you?"

"I think the question is, how are *you?*"

"Getting by."

"Meggie, if there's anything—" he began.

She didn't know what gave her the courage. But she heard herself saying, "There is."

Zach leaned closer. "Name it."

And she did. "I have to speak with Nate."

Zach blinked—and retreated from her a little in his chair.

She refused to drop her gaze as she asked carefully, "If I were to fly to L.A., would I find him in the phone book, do you think?"

Zach frowned. "Meggie..."

"You asked me if there was anything you could do.

And there is—you can answer my question. Can I find Nate's number in the L.A. phone book?''

Zach was still frowning, but he told her what she needed to know. "Bravo Investigative Services. It's in the Yellow Pages."

She nodded. "Thank you."

He shrugged, then held out a hand. "Come on. Put your worries behind you for a while and let's have a dance."

"Oh, Zach. You're kind. But I just don't feel much like dancing."

He dropped his hand. "I understand." He glanced away, off toward the dance floor—and then beyond it, to where Edna Heller and Tess DeMarley stood on the sidelines together.

Meggie saw the way his gaze lingered on Tess. She suggested lightly, "I see Tess DeMarley over there. You might ask her."

Zach looked at Meggie again and grinned. He had a charming grin—but then, all the Bravos did. "I'm working up the nerve."

Meggie stood to go. "Good luck," she said softly.

He stared up at her for a long, slow time before he replied, "Same to you."

* * * * *

Could Meggie have a chance with Nate after all? To find out, look for Meggie and Nate's story in Book II of Christine Rimmer's CONVENIENTLY YOURS miniseries. It's called MARRIAGE BY NECESSITY and it's coming in March 1998, only from Silhouette Special Edition.

Take 4 bestselling love stories FREE

Plus get a FREE surprise gift!

Welcome to the Towers!

In January
New York Times bestselling author

NORA ROBERTS

takes us to the fabulous Maine coast mansion
haunted by a generations-old secret and introduces
us to the fascinating family that lives there.

Mechanic Catherine "C.C." Calhoun and hotel magnate
Trenton St. James mix like axle grease and mineral
water—until they kiss. Efficient Amanda Calhoun finds
easygoing Sloan O'Riley insufferable—and irresistible.
And they all must race to solve the mystery
surrounding a priceless hidden emerald necklace.

Catherine and Amanda

THE Calhoun Women

**A special 2-in-1 edition containing
COURTING CATHERINE and A MAN FOR AMANDA.**

Look for the next installment of
THE CALHOUN WOMEN with Lilah and Suzanna's
stories, coming in March 1998.

Available at your favorite retail outlet.

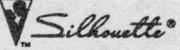

SUSAN MALLERY

Continues the twelve-book
series—36 HOURS—in
January 1998 with
Book Seven

THE RANCHER AND THE RUNAWAY BRIDE

When Randi Howell fled the altar, she'd been running for her
life! And she'd kept on running—straight into the arms of
rugged rancher Brady Jones. She knew he had his suspicions,
but how could she tell him the truth about her identity? Then
again, if she ever wanted to approach the altar in earnest, how
could she not?

For Brady and Randi and *all* the residents of Grand Springs,
Colorado, the storm-induced blackout was just the beginning
of 36 Hours that changed *everything!* You won't want to
miss a single book.

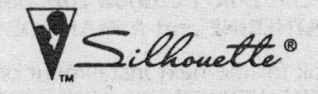

Available at your favorite retail outlet.

Look us up on-line at: http://www.romance.net   36HRS7

Coming this December 1997 from

Silhouette SPECIAL EDITION

*AND BABY
MAKES THREE:
THE NEXT
GENERATION:*

*The Adams women of Texas
all find love—and
motherhood—in the most
unexpected ways!*

The Adams family of Texas returns!
Bestselling author **Sherryl Woods** continues
the saga in these irresistible new books.
Don't miss the first three titles in the series:

In December 1997: **THE LITTLEST ANGEL** (SE #1142)
When Angela Adams told Clint Brady she was pregnant, she
was decidedly displeased with the rancher's reaction. Could
Clint convince Angela he wanted them to be a family?

In February 1998: **NATURAL BORN TROUBLE** (SE #1156)
Dani Adams resisted when single dad Duke Jenkins claimed
she'd be the perfect mother for his sons. But Dani was
captivated by the boys—and their sexy father!

In May 1998: **UNEXPECTED MOMMY** (SE #1171)
To claim his share of the White Pines ranch, Chance Adams
tried to seduce his uncle's lovely stepdaughter. But then he
fell in love with Jenny Adams for real....

Available at your favorite retail outlet.

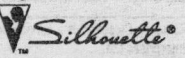

As seen on TV!
Free Gift Offer

With a Free Gift proof-of-purchase from any Silhouette® book, you can receive a beautiful cubic zirconia pendant.

This gorgeous marquise-shaped stone is a genuine cubic zirconia—accented by an 18" gold tone necklace.

(Approximate retail value $19.95)

Send for yours today...
compliments of ▼ *Silhouette*®

To receive your free gift, a cubic zirconia pendant, send us one original proof-of-purchase, photocopies not accepted, from the back of any Silhouette Romance™, Silhouette Desire®, Silhouette Special Edition®, Silhouette Intimate Moments® or Silhouette Yours Truly™ title available at your favorite retail outlet, together with the Free Gift Certificate, plus a check or money order for $1.65 U.S./$2.15 CAN. (do not send cash) to cover postage and handling, payable to Silhouette Free Gift Offer. We will send you the specified gift. Allow 6 to 8 weeks for delivery. Offer good until March 31, 1998, or while quantities last. Offer valid in the U.S. and Canada only.

Free Gift Certificate

Name: _____

Address: _____

City: _____ State/Province: _____ Zip/Postal Code: _____

Mail this certificate, one proof-of-purchase and a check or money order for postage and handling to: SILHOUETTE FREE GIFT OFFER 1998. In the U.S.: 3010 Walden Avenue, P.O. Box 9077, Buffalo, NY 14269-9077. In Canada: P.O. Box 613, Fort Erie, Ontario L2Z 5X3.

FREE GIFT OFFER
084-KFD

ONE PROOF-OF-PURCHASE

To collect your fabulous FREE GIFT, a cubic zirconia pendant, you must include this original proof-of-purchase for each gift with the properly completed Free Gift Certificate.

084-KFDR2

RETURN TO WHITEHORN

Silhouette's beloved **MONTANA MAVERICKS** returns with brand-new stories from your favorite authors! Welcome back to Whitehorn, Montana—a place where rich tales of passion and adventure are unfolding under the Big Sky. The new generation of Mavericks will leave you breathless!

Coming from Silhouette Special Edition°:

February 98: LETTER TO A LONESOME COWBOY by Jackie Merritt

March 98: WIFE MOST WANTED by Joan Elliott Pickart

May 98: A FATHER'S VOW by Myrna Temte

June 98: A HERO'S HOMECOMING by Laurie Paige

And don't miss these two very special additions to the Montana Mavericks saga:

MONTANA MAVERICKS WEDDINGS
by Diana Palmer, Ann Major and Susan Mallery
Short story collection available April 98

WILD WEST WIFE by Susan Mallery
Harlequin Historicals available July 98

Round up these great new stories
at your favorite retail outlet.